Secrets

of the

Dark

Closet

GAYLE LARSON SCHUCK

ISBN 978-0-578-66447-7 (Second Edition)

Front cover photo by Leah Meisch Photography

Copyright © 2020 by Gayle Larson Schuck
All rights reserved. No part of this publication may be reproduced, distributed, or transmitted in any form or by any means, including photocopying, recording, or other electronic or mechanical methods without the prior written permission of the publisher. For permission requests, solicit the publisher via the address below.

Printed in the United States of America

A person goes through life making one choice after another.
How can you tell if a choice will take you
down a road you do not want to go?

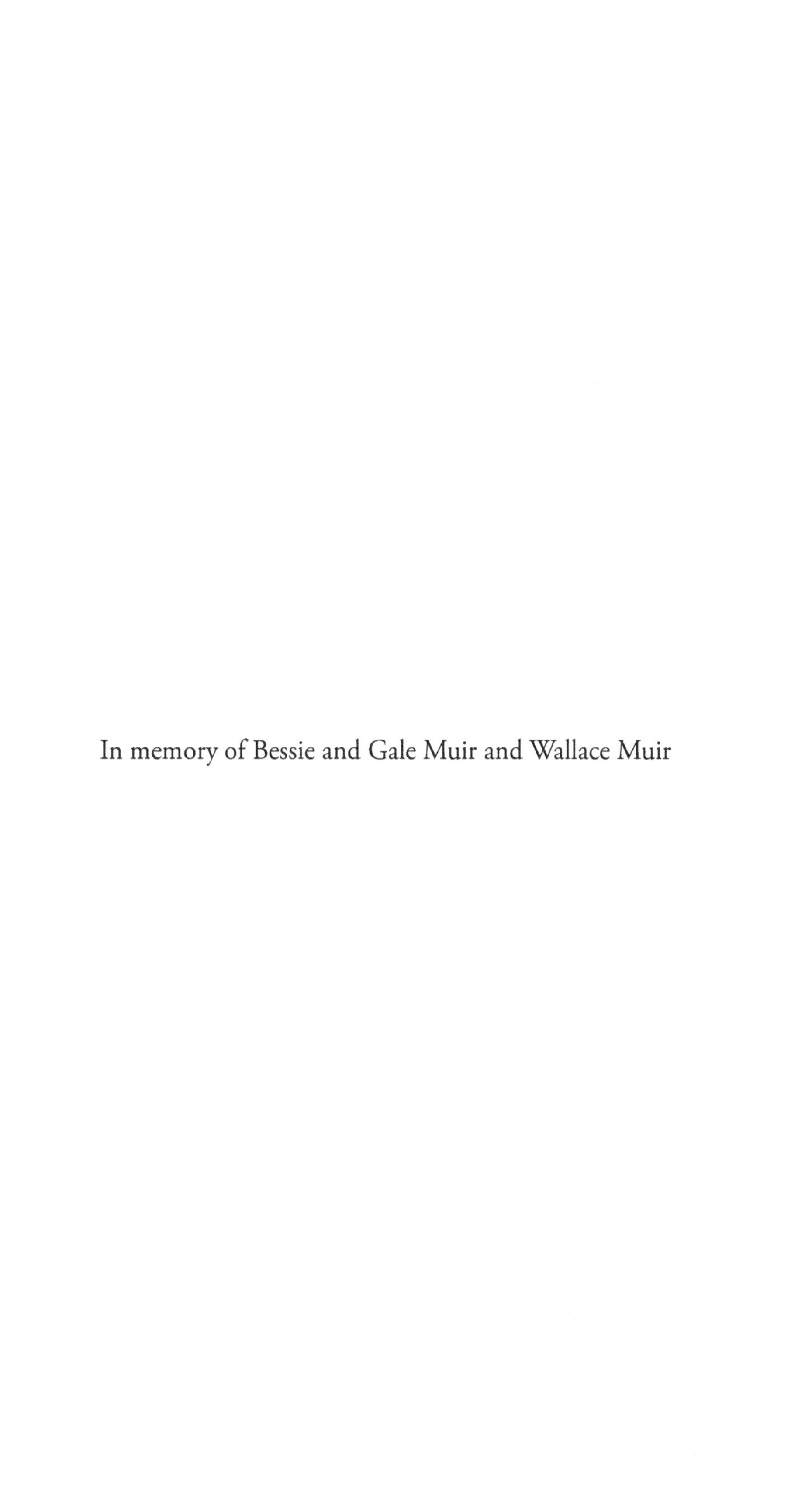

In memory of Bessie and Gale Muir and Wallace Muir

Acknowledgments

One cannot spend years writing a book without reference materials. Thank you to the following publications, places, and people:

- *Muir-Kloubec Genealogy and History from 1708 to 2005*, by Wallace Muir
- Muir-Kloubec photos copied and preserved by Willis Muir
- Webster County Museum, Fort Dodge, Iowa
- Webster County Courthouse, Fort Dodge, Iowa
- LaMoure Chronicle *Yesterdays* column, LaMoure, North Dakota
- *The History of LaMoure 1882–1982*
- Oral history by Carrie Kloubec Brandes, circa 1980
- North Dakota State Library
- Bismarck Veterans Memorial Public Library
- The recollections of my aunts and uncles, siblings, cousins, second cousins, nieces, and nephews have been very valuable.

Special thanks to early readers of the manuscripts: Andy Lindberg, Sandi Bennett, Jean Rath, Sonja Erickson, Sherry Garner, Jane Sbragia, and Muriel Keller, and to Cinnamon Schuck who did the final proofing.

A mere thank you seems inadequate for the professional assistance of Jordis Conrad, Barbara Brabec, and Colleen Parker; prayer support from Sandi Bennett, Kristi Simenson, Julia Goei, and friends at church; and moral support of the Dakota Writers and countless others who helped me finish the task; and to my best encourager, Larry Schuck, for whom this has become a long adventure. As Bessie might say, "Land's sake, you are the best!"

Author's Note

Secrets of the Dark Closet is a work of historical fiction based on legal documentation. While family names are authentic, the stories are purely a product of the author's imagination.

Documented facts and anecdotes are explained in the chapter notes at the back of the book.

Characters

Bessie Emma Kloubec is the central character. Bessie is eleven years old when the story opens. She is the third of six children and the oldest daughter in the family.

Vincent Kloubec, Bessie's father, was born in Bohemia and moved to the United States with his family when he was four in 1864. The family settled at Cedar Rapids, Iowa.

Mary Spirek Kloubec, Bessie's mother, was born in Bohemia and moved to the United States with her family when she was eleven months old. The Spirek clan settled near Iowa City, Iowa, for a time and later moved west to Webster County near Fort Dodge.

George Kloubec, Bessie's oldest brother, was fifteen at the turn of the century.

Joseph Kloubec, a brother who possibly had epilepsy, was two years older than Bessie.

Carrie Kloubec, Bessie's only sister, was two years younger than Bessie.

Edwin (Eddie) Kloubec, Bessie's brother, was four years younger than she was.

Bill Kloubec, Bessie's youngest brother, was five years younger than she was.

Anna Spirek, known as Babi in the book, was Bessie's maternal grandmother.

Al Roots was Mary Spirek Kloubec's second husband.

Gale Muir was twenty-two when he moved from Jackson, Minnesota, to LaMoure, North Dakota, to farm with his parents. Several of his siblings also moved to the area.

Robert Crawford Muir was Gale's father.

Mary McLean Muir was Gale's mother.

Anton and Annie Spirek were Mary Spirek Kloubec's brother and sister-in-law.

Charles and Anna Spirek were another brother and sister-in-law to Mary Spirek Kloubec.

Anna and Joseph Koll were Mary Spirek Kloubec's younger sister and her husband.

Introduction

Grandma Bessie was sixty-one when I was born toward the middle of her thirty-one grandchildren. An apron-clad sprite with a droll sense of humor, Bessie's cookie jar was always full and her tire swing and lawn cart ready for use by energetic children. I can still see her bending over in her flower garden, watering the delicate blooms with rainwater scooped from a twenty-gallon stone jar. To this day, we cousins agree she was the perfect grandmother.

Back then, none of us dreamed that Bessie had secrets. We didn't know her world was shattered, her family shamed and scattered when she was a young girl. Although she died in 1966, it wasn't until the 1980s that one of her sons, Wallace Muir, began to uncover documents revealing the facts of her growing-up years.

Rumors had clung to the family like the scent of mothballs in a storage room. The clues were there too, if only we'd paid attention. For instance, my Presbyterian grandmother gave me a very old triangular veil, but it didn't occur to me then that she might have worn it to attend Catholic mass.

The little closet located off her kitchen, known in the family as the "dark closet," became a symbol to me of the mystery surrounding her life. That symbol was enhanced a few years ago when a cousin revealed that an old handgun had been found in the closet after Bessie's death.

Wallace Muir recorded the facts in the *Muir-Kloubec Genealogy and History 1708–2005*, which made me wonder what it was like for Bessie to grow up in a disintegrating family. To find out, I lived in Bessie's skin for about ten years and wrote the story as she might have told it fifty to sixty years after the events.

My husband and I made two trips to Iowa doing further research. We visited the Webster County Courthouse, drove the chalk-white roads past farms where Bessie or her relatives lived, and walked among the tall gravestones in Graceland Cemetery.

One day as we drove Highway 20 on the way to Moorland, where part of the family lived for four years, we happened past a red brick institution. We pulled in and looked around. It was now a Baptist seminary, but a sign explained that one tall brick building was the original Webster County Poor Farm. We'd accidently found the place where my great-grandfather had spent his final days.

Moments later, we passed a large pink billboard with SECRETS written in large letters. I could hardly speak. "Secrets" was the working title I'd chosen for this book.

There is a great deal of personal angst in telling this story. After all, would Bessie want her "dirty laundry" aired even now, over one hundred years after the events took place? But times have changed. We no longer hide the kinds of things she found shameful.

Never one to take herself seriously, I can almost hear her chuckling at the thought of anyone wanting to write about her. Yet she remains an example of courage and strength for today's generation, a woman of simplicity, bravery, and quiet confidence.

—Gayle Larson Schuck

Prologue

Eleven is a disastrous age, an in-between time, like when you jump across a creek and wonder midair whether you will splash into the water or land on the other side. It is like the hour before dawn when night still casts its mystery and the lamp of daylight has not yet been turned up. Yes, and eleven is also like a caterpillar that suddenly turns into a butterfly but has no schoolbook teaching it how to fly into another world.

Neither were there instructions for unfolding my wings at eleven. When I was ten, I knew my place. There I was, standing poker-faced in the family photo with my siblings and parents. I sat at the children's table during holiday dinners and whiled away summer afternoons making hollyhock dolls. My skirt was shorter so I could run bases with ease as my molasses-colored braids slapped at my back. In the evening, Father tucked me under his arm as he read the *Slova Amerik'y*.

By the time I turned twelve, I found myself carrying the responsibilities of a grown-up. I had graduated to long swishy skirts and listened around the corner as the future of my family was settled over coffee and kolaches. By twelve, the family photo from age ten had been burned in the trash. And Father's chair sat emptier than if he'd died.

All those changes took place when I was eleven and zigzagging through the year like a beginner butterfly. Does a butterfly ever want to go back to its cozy cocoon? How does it find the courage to go on if the milkweed stems that nourished it are broken? Where does a butterfly find rest?

Oh, the secret lives of butterflies have nothing on the secrets of my family, those from when I was eleven and those that happened later. Our family shed our members and our past like a butterfly shedding its cocoon. We locked our memories away in a dark closet, hoping they would never be discovered by the generation yet to come.

PART I

1

April 1899

"Happy Birthday, Bessie." I expected to hear those words on my eleventh birthday. I also hoped for spice cake with thick brown sugar frosting and maybe a present or two.

Instead, the day's events flung me from a fairly happy childhood into a mysterious and violent grown-up world. By the end of that day, I would have settled for even one person remembering my birthday.

Sometime after midnight, I had awakened to a strange silence. My room was as black as Iowa mud. Faint gray light from the tall, narrow window was the only relief from the darkness. My heart beat fast as I lay still, listening beyond my sister Carrie's whiffled breath.

Finally, I heard a low scraping rumble. Across the farmyard, someone was pushing the barn door open on its rusty rollers. I slipped out of bed and went to the window, the night chill wrapping its arms around my white nightie. Moments passed. The rumble rose again, followed by a *thunk* I knew well. Someone had thrown the wooden latch into place.

Seconds ticked by as slow as an unwinding clock. *Tick. Tick. Tick.* Blood pumped hard through my body like water rushing down a drain spout. What was happening? Was there a thief outside? Why had Mutt not barked?

A shadowy figure passed below the window, a horse and rider going at a slow trot. The man adjusted something behind him and then pulled his hat down, a familiar action I had seen my father do all my life. Within a few seconds, the clopping of the horse's hooves on the gravel faded, and the man and horse vanished into the foggy night.

I watched a bit longer, my elbows hugging the warm patches they had made on the windowsill. Then Mutt came into view. He sat on his haunches and whimpered, staring after the shadowy rider.

From the other side of the bedroom wall, I heard another sound, like the high mewing of an abandoned kitten protesting in fear or pain. My feet seemed stuck to the floor where I stood shivering by the window, but my hand reached out and grabbed the shawl from a hook on the nearby wall.

Then a wail, half howl, came from the other side of the wall. Carrie, who was almost nine, stirred in our bed but did not wake. My heartbeat thundered. I had never heard such a sound before, but it could only be one thing: the anguished cries of my mother. I covered my mouth, the shawl dropping to the floor.

My mother was a big, rawboned woman with little use for nonsense. She was only twelve when she cooked for the Spirek wagon train that brought the family's cattle and goods to western Iowa. She could do almost anything, from sewing our dresses and britches to shocking corn. She was handsome rather than pretty, imposing rather than delicate. I had never heard her cry. Until now.

Finally, my feet felt free to move. I scooped up the shawl and felt my way to the bedroom door and down the hall. My parents' room was off-limits to us kids, so I seldom went there except to put away laundry. We never crawled into bed with our parents if we were frightened or sick or could not sleep. Instead, we six kids tiptoed to each other's rooms and comforted each other.

Now I decided to break the rule and enter my parents' room, propelled by concern and a little curiosity. If Mother were crying, my fear and possible punishment seemed a small waterdrop in the creek compared to what was wrong.

I took a deep breath and opened the door to their bedroom. A chimney lamp cast wavy shadows on the cabbage rose wallpaper. My mother lay crumpled in the mahogany bed, a hanky clutched to her face. I leaned over her.

"There now, there now," I said as I did when comforting my little brothers. I patted her arm. Her wailing increased. My baby brothers did that too, I reasoned, crying harder when they thought someone was listening. Crawling in bed next to Mother, I drew up the quilt around us. After several minutes, she quieted down, although her shudders still shook the bed.

When her sniffling increased again, I eased out of bed and opened the top bureau drawer where I had placed her freshly ironed hankies. Grabbing a couple, I handed them to her and crawled back under the covers.

"Bessie, where's Vincent?" she finally managed to ask in a mangled voice. The question startled me because she used his first name instead of saying "your father."

"Father left on his horse." Some kids at school called their parents Pa and Ma, while others used the more affectionate Mama and Papa, but we were too proper for those names.

Mother turned, and I saw the bruising on her left cheek for the first time.

I cried in a loud whisper, "Mother, what happened?"

"This is the worst," she said, dabbing at her cheek. It was hard to see in the dim light, but the whole side of her face looked black and blue. "His back hurt so much today. I could hardly bear to watch him suffer so." Mother's speech sounded a bit mealy, and she spoke out of one side of her mouth.

"But then he disappeared for hours, and I feared the worst. I was already asleep tonight when he stumbled on the stairs. When he tripped over the chair, I had enough! I sat straight up in bed and said, 'You're drunker than Cooter Brown!' He came right over and hit me so hard everything went black!" Mother said, touching her cheek.

Her eyes roamed the room. I looked around too and noticed things out of place. The straight-backed chair lay on its side, a picture hung askew on the wall, and clothing was thrown hither and thither.

"Bessie, bring me the basin," Mother stated as she poked her tongue around in her mouth.

Standing at the basin, my back to Mother, I looked in the mirror and formed an *O* with my eyes and mouth and shook my hands.

Mother was confiding in me as though I were grown-up! If only the circumstance was not so grim.

I took the basin back to the bed. Mother fished around in her mouth and then spit a bloody tooth into the basin. I stared at the tooth, an eyetooth, then at Mother's wound. Looking at the swelling flesh of her cheek made my stomach queasy. Moving slowly, I dumped the tooth in the wastebasket and poured a little icy water into the basin from the pitcher on the wash table.

At first, I gingerly held the cloth to her cheek. After a few minutes, I tried to put salve on it, but she turned and began spitting more blood into the basin. When she looked up at me, she must have seen my discomfort because she finished the repair job herself.

Afterward, I crawled in bed next to her, and Mother gripped my little hand in her big rough one. Her hands had been a symbol of strength to me, but now she drew strength from me.

Eventually, Mother drifted into an uneasy sleep, but I lay awake thinking.

***

A person goes through life making one choice after another. How can you tell if a choice will take you down a road you do not want to go? Our family had been happy when I was little. We rented a farm in Elkhorn Township, where so many of my Spirek aunts and uncles lived. However, like everyone else, my parents were anxious to own land.

My relatives loved America and were eager to adopt her ways. In school, we children were told, "Now we live in America. We will speak English, not Bohemian!" They relished the freedom and opportunity of America, especially the right to vote, own land, and attend public meetings. These things were denied them in the old country.

When a farm near Callender in Fulton Township came up for sale, Father and Mother pulled together enough money for a down payment. It was a pretty place, with Hardin Creek running through it and more trees than in Elkhorn Township. Their excitement ran so high! I will never forget the day they signed papers to buy the land. They danced a jig in the kitchen, knocking over the water pitcher.

The broken glass and spilt water did not bother any of us then, but now I wondered if it was an omen. Much more had been shattered since then.

The move was difficult. Made in an early fall storm, the dirt roads were slick with mud, and a fierce wind pushed against the wagons the whole way. Our "new" farm needed a lot of work. Both Father and Mother spent long days laboring with it. I was eight, and Carrie was six. We watched over our little brothers and did what we could in the house. Sometimes my uncles came over to help, but they had their own farms to tend. And now they lived miles away.

Maybe it was because Father was bone-weary and not paying attention, but one day a horse kicked him good in the head and back. He dragged himself to the house and took to bed for almost a week. We kids could hear him moaning in pain, but even then, Mother did not allow us in the bedroom.

He was still pale with pain when he decided he had lain around enough. He was determined not to lose any more work time. He hobbled back outside, but something had changed in him, something more than the sad bend of his body.

He began to yell at us kids for no good reason. He was mean to the animals too, once kicking Mutt so hard he flew through the air. He cursed Mother out a lot and complained about everything.

One day our neighbor, Tader Smith, stopped by and brought a bottle meant to help with the pain. Father started taking a glassful at night so he could sleep. Then he began drinking before supper. Finally, he began keeping a bottle in the barn.

I do not remember Father ever hurting Mother before that night, though I had sometimes wondered how she got so many bruises. She grew to have a look in her eyes I had never seen before, just like Mutt the day after Father kicked him.

Those were my thoughts as I lay awake through the early morning of my eleventh birthday, with Mother clutching my hand.

2

I fell asleep toward morning, not waking until the sun splashed across my face. It felt very strange to wake up in my parents' bed, but then I remembered what had happened. Mother was up and at it already.

A sick feeling settled into the pit of my stomach, and I half-heartedly rolled out of bed. I smoothed the covers, tucking them neatly under the pillows, and then hurried to the room I shared with Carrie. She too was up and gone. I pulled on a cotton dress and fresh apron.

Rushing down the stairs, I spied Carrie, who stood on tiptoes stirring porridge at the black cook stove. We had learned our way around the kitchen as soon as we could stand on a stool to dry dishes or stir a pot.

"Well, I guess you got your beauty sleep," commented Carrie, who was maddeningly snoopy. I chose to ignore her remark, certain it was a hint that she knew something was amiss.

"Where's Mother?" I asked.

"She and the boys are out doing chores."

"Have you seen Father?" I probed.

"No," Carrie said as she stared into the porridge. "What happened last night?"

I shrugged. "Father took off on his horse in the middle of the night, and Mother—"

Just then, the kitchen door burst open, and Mother walked in carrying the egg basket. She wore her cotton work bonnet. Usually it kept her hair clean and neat, but today it also hid those awful bruises. George, who was fifteen, came in behind her carrying a pail of milk.

Before the door closed, I glimpsed my younger brothers, Eddie and Bill, out in the yard playing tag with Joe.

I put my head down to avoid eye contact with Carrie. Mother often chastised us for giving "looks" to each other. Rolling our eyes was practically a felony. I went to the cupboard and pulled out bowls to set the table.

Mother tapped her chin with her index finger. "Put plates down too, Bessie," she ordered me. "We'll scramble some eggs. And don't bother setting a place for your father." She turned and began skimming cream off the top of the milk and putting it in a pint-sized pitcher. Then she poured the milk into a larger white ceramic pitcher.

Carrie looked at me out the corner of her eye, struggling to contain her curiosity.

Mother cracked eggs into a bowl, then added milk from the pitcher and whisked them together. I took the heavy cast iron skillet off its hook on the wall and put it on the stove. Then I took a loaf of bread from the breadbox and began cutting thick slices.

"George, take the extra milk out and put it in the cooler. This time, be sure to place the cloth cover on it," Mother commanded as she poured the eggs into the pan. George already sat at the oak table hungrily watching us prepare breakfast, but he got up and trudged out the door carrying the milk pail.

I had been helping with kitchen duties for as long as I could remember, and I practically grew up burping babies on my shoulder. In the past few months, I had outgrown the sleeves on my shirtwaists, and my skirts barely reached my high-top boots. But last night, I had helped Mother, and that really made me feel grown-up.

Smugly I thought, now I understood why adults protected children from bad news. Really, Carrie, Eddie, and Bill, not to mention Joe, should not have to know about last night's horrible events. Carrie would not coax me into giving away any secrets.

"Bessie Emma! Mind those eggs!" Mother yelled. My mind jumped back to the present, and I pushed the frying pan to the cooler center part of the stove. Mother only used my middle name when she was upset.

About that time, my brothers rushed through the door. They pretended to wash their hands in the basin of soapy water we kept by the door and scooted into their seats at the table with much scraping of chairs. Once the food was on the table and we were all seated, Mother crossed herself, and we became silent.

"Our Father, who art in heaven," Mother began, leading us in the Pater Noster, the Lord's Prayer. It was Sunday, after all. Saying the prayer together at breakfast on Sunday mornings was our way of going to church now that we lived so far from Fort Dodge. Even so, this was a strange Sunday. Father was gone, and I did not know where he was.

As the prayer ended, I looked up and caught my breath. I had not noticed Mother removing her bonnet. Now the red and purple wound on her cheek made me suck in my breath. The others gawked at Mother as if she were a two-headed cow. Mother put her hand to her cheek.

"An accident. 'Tis nothing that won't heal," she said sternly.

No one dared ask what had happened. We picked up our forks and ate in uneasy silence. As soon as possible, the boys left the table. I could not remember the last time they had left without eating every bite put before them, but I understood how they felt because nothing tasted very good that day.

I figured how my siblings might react to the obvious problem in our family. The boys' rooms were over the kitchen and faced the barnyard. George may have even seen Father saddle his horse and ride away during the night. Still, he would not get too excited. He might even find a humorous spin on the whole incident. Today, as I expected, he went upstairs to nap.

Carrie would spend every moment trying to find out what happened from Mother or me.

Eddie was seven and the most tenderhearted of us kids. He loved to scratch away on an old fiddle someone had given him, and he enjoyed reading. When he saw Mother's bruised face, he looked like someone had punched him in the stomach. After breakfast, he went to the parlor and sat looking out the window.

Baby Bill did not much like my name for him anymore. After all, he was five years old. My parents were relieved to put him in school early, and he did very well. He was full of energy, a real lovable rascal. He got more spankings than the rest of us, but he was also the most fun. Today he went upstairs dragging his old blanket with him.

Then there was Joe. No doubt, he added to Father and Mother's problems. Joe was two years older than me, but his mind never grew up. He had fits. He would fall on the floor, foam at the mouth, and thrash around. Afterward, he was all worn out, and we would put him in his narrow little bed.

They had tried to put Joe in school, but the teacher said to keep him home after he had fallen out of his desk with a fit and upended the coal bucket. All the students rushed to a corner while Carrie and I put a ruler between his teeth so he would not swallow his tongue. Joe could not learn much anyway. We had to watch him every moment, but he was earnest and sweet, and we all loved him.

Today Joe asked to go out to his "farm," which was a fenced area where he could play safely. He carried his favorite toy, a little wooden soldier.

"Bessie, take Joe outside," Mother ordered. "Carrie will help me clean up the kitchen."

I took Joe out, and he solemnly dug in the dirt with an old hoe Father had given him. He had propped his toy soldier against the fence to watch him.

So many times, I had asked God to help Joe. I loved him so much. If he could do sums like George or read a book like Eddie, it would have meant everything to me. I also had a selfish reason for wanting him to be normal; I was tired of taking care of a boy who was taller than me. Why, he was beginning to grow chin hair.

"Father go! Father go!" Joe began saying as he dug in the dirt.

"What did you say, Joe?"

"Father go last night. He mad at me!"

"Why do you say that?" I questioned, surprised that Joe knew something of last night's events. But he only repeated the same words over and over.

Finally I said, "Joe, Father isn't mad at you. He's just grumpy since his accident."

"He go. Not come back," Joe said sadly. Then he focused on his project and seemed to forget about Father.

I sat close by for a while then locked the gate to the fence and wandered to the nearby stand of trees. Between Joe's "field" and the little shelterbelt, Mother's garden stretched out in long rows. It was early yet, and we had only planted peas, onions, and potatoes so far. The little green plants were just poking through the ground. Mother worked hard at gardening, but it was a work of love and not a chore. Every year she ordered new kinds of seeds and seedlings. She was the first in the area to plant apricot trees, which grew on the far side of the garden.

I preferred flowers to vegetables. Soon I hoped to plant the four-o'clock and zinnia seeds we'd harvested the year before. We had trays of tomato seedlings growing in the sewing room windows waiting for the ground to warm.

In the shelterbelt, blooming apricot, plum, apple, and choke-cherry trees gave off a fragrance that eased the mind and heart. How could things be so bad when the sun shone bright, the birds sang, and the air smelled like heaven itself?

The trees hid one of my favorite places, the creek that ran on the other side. I would sneak off to the creek by myself as often as possible. I loved to sit on a little log bench and watch the water drift by as I thought through the important things in life and had my little talks with God.

Today, I leaned forward and held a stick in the water. Watching the quick spring current flow around it, I had an odd feeling of standing in a doorway between childhood and being grown-up. For a minute, I wanted to return to the past and remain a girl. Then I thought of Joe, who would never grow up, and realized I did not have much choice.

I had plum forgot it was my birthday until that moment. No one else had mentioned it either, with all the strange things going on. I already knew I did not like being eleven. It felt heavy, like a canvas draped over my shoulders.

Reluctantly, I backtracked through the trees and checked on Joe. He seemed content to dig in the dirt, so I went back to the house dragging my bare feet across the soft blanket of chamomile. I planned to mention my birthday, but when I walked in the house, Carrie was pushing Mother for answers.

"Where did Father go?" Carrie's tone carried a bit of a challenge, I thought uneasily.

"I don't know. And I don't care if he ever comes back," Mother declared. She sat on a kitchen chair, her chin held high, her voice bitter. She reminded me of a cat that falls off a fence and then walks away with its tail in the air.

Mother did not fool me. She wanted Father to come back. Our family was knit together by hard work, close quarters, and isolation. I could not even imagine life without Father.

"What happened?" Carrie asked quickly, before the chance to quiz Mother disappeared.

"He was drinking. It makes him go mad." Mother seemed to search through her memories. "He just came at me and hit me as hard as he could," she said, dry-eyed.

I was shocked and miffed that Mother was telling any of this to Carrie. After all, I was the mature one. Carrie was too young to hear such things.

"Mother, we need help. Let me take the team and buggy to Uncle Anton's," I begged.

Father had taken Ozzy, the gentle riding horse. I knew I could not ride Buck, who had earned his name. But, if I finally got to drive Mother's horse and buggy, I would be the heroine going for help.

"No," Mother replied, touching her cheek. "I don't want them to know."

She did not seem too certain, so I grabbed my shoes and stockings, ready to go anyway.

"You see," Mother said quietly, and I stopped still. "If we spill the beans to the rest of the family, then your Father will find out, and he'll really be mad. We don't want to do any more to get his anger started." A puzzled look creased her forehead as she touched her cheek again, as though she wanted to remember what she had done to bring on his anger the night before.

It did not seem to me that she had done anything to deserve having her face black and blue, but maybe she was right. Maybe he would be sorry for what he did. Maybe we could find a doctor who could fix his back pain. Maybe this would not happen again.

I looked out the window and saw a rainstorm brewing in the west. When lightning cracked through the sky, I bolted out the door to shepherd Joe into the house. We spent the rest of that day in the gloom of a rainy spring day. I could not bring myself to mention what day it was. Happy birthday, Bessie.

3

May 1899

Father came home a couple of days later. He did not apologize to Mother, as far as I know. For a few days, we all acted like we had before my birthday, except everyone was on tippy-toes trying not to upset things.

I remembered when we had looked up to our wise, funny, hardworking father. Now when he was around, we tried to become invisible, afraid we might say or do something to set him off. Even Joe knew to stay away from Father when he drank. Father sometimes sat and muttered about how Joe was useless and dangerous and ate too much food. One day he said the best thing to do was to send Joe away. I was shocked! Send him away? I wondered what he meant but didn't dare ask any questions.

Spring is a busy time on a farm. Along with cleaning up the muck of winter, everything from calves to kittens was being born, and there were crops to plant. Mother and George hustled from dawn to dusk, trying to get all the work done. Meanwhile, Father now drank openly, took off whenever he wanted to, and generally was not any help at all.

The tension was as thick as overcooked corn meal. A week after my birthday, Joe had been talking endlessly, when Father grabbed him, pinned him to the wall and told him to shut his mouth. The veins in his neck pumped and his fist worked, ready to ball up and punch Joe.

And, as if we needed a reminder of all our problems, it was taking Mother's cheek a long time to heal. We could see the swelling and bruising there, but not the tender inside of her mouth. Her mealy speech revealed that it hurt. While she healed, she stayed at home, sending George to town to sell eggs and cream at the general store.

My worst day that spring came when Father decided I was not going to school anymore. It was early May, and I was almost finished with sixth grade. We usually walked to school, which was a quarter-mile south of the farm, across Hardin Creek. I enjoyed the walk, especially in the spring. As usual, Carrie fussed the whole way about a spelling test, and Eddie stumbled along with his nose in the McGuffey's Reader. Bill tossed pieces of the gypsum rock that covered the white, dusty road. I would be looking for every sign of flowers in the ditch.

One morning Father was going to Fort Dodge, so we decided to catch a ride with him. When I started to climb into the wagon, he looked down at me, stuck out his foot, and pushed me to the ground!

"You're too old for book learning!" he said. "Your Mother needs you at home." I just lay sprawled out on the ground in shock. Bill, Eddie, and Carrie looked over the side of the wagon box with surprise on their faces. As the wagon moved forward, Carrie grimaced at me. None of us knew what to think.

I picked myself up, went in the house, and told Mother what had happened. She put her hands on her hips and pursed her lips. "Well, you better help me finish the washing then," she said.

I turned and ran up the stairs to the room I shared with Carrie. Face down on the bed, I cried because I liked school and did not want to quit. I cried out of confusion over what was happening to Father. I cried because my behind still hurt where I had landed so hard. Moreover, I cried because Mother had not shown one bit of sympathy for me.

That night when Carrie and I went to our room, there was a package lying on the bed. We exchanged bewildered looks before Carrie bounded over and picked it up.

"It says 'To Bessie.'" She looked at me a long moment, the wheels turning in her head. "Oh, Bessie, none of us even remembered your birthday," she said, remorse written on her face. She handed the package to me.

I held it a moment before untying the green ribbon and loosening the white tissue paper. A photo album was inside. Not just a plain brown one, but one with a lock and a green and cream-colored leather cover. It was embossed with flowers and swirls. I stroked the green velvet of the back cover. The board pages would hold all our photos and many more in years to come.

I rubbed my behind, remembering what had happened this morning. Instinctively I knew Mother gave me the album because she cared about what had happened today. It also showed me she was afraid to confront Father about my school attendance. Mother was in very deep trouble. That insight made me pause. I had always expected so much from my parents, but maybe they were just grown-up kids trying to get along in this world.

Carrie handed me a pencil, and I wrote on the inside cover, "Miss Bessie Kloubec, Callender, Iowa." I did not want to put down the current date because I hadn't received it on my birthday and that memory still stung, so I wrote, "December 25, 1899." Perhaps by December, our family troubles would be gone.

During the night, I listened to my parents argue for a long time. Then Father left again. This time he did not come back.

4

May 1899

Father used to say the good Lord rested after six days of work and we should too. On Sundays, we did not do much work beyond taking care of the animals and making meals.

Once breakfast was over, the boys went to their rooms or outside. Carrie and I liked to hide away in the sewing room. Before long, either company would arrive or our family would hitch up the wagon to go visit relatives.

Mother came from a big family, and most of them lived in Webster County. We saw the most of Uncle Charles and Uncle Anton and their families. They both married girls named Anna, so we called Charles's wife Aunt Anna and Anton's wife Aunt Annie. When our three families got together, there were seventeen children to play with. However, since Mother's "accident" on my birthday, we had not seen any of them, and Father was still absent.

The first Sunday in May, I cleaned up the kitchen by myself after breakfast. I filled the dishpan from the reservoir on the cook stove, shaved some homemade soap into the water, and quickly washed the dishes. After everything was tidy, I took the extra eggs to cool in the cellar. Then I slipped into the parlor, a small room decorated with red upholstered mahogany furniture. Through the curtain covering the doorway, I could see Carrie in the sewing room hunched over her latest book, *Kidnapped.*

"Oh, pooh," I said, flopping into a chair and looking at the wallpaper we had so carefully hung. Our family's problems seemed to tumble down on me every time I had a spare moment to think. What was going to happen to us?

Lost in thought, I finally became aware that Mutt was barking. Uncle Charles's wagon was coming up the driveway, and his whole family was along. Suddenly I realized there were tears on my face. I pulled out my hanky and wiped my face dry, then practiced a smile for my mouth.

"Mother! Carrie! We've got company!" I shouted. Carrie put her book down, and we ran outside to greet everyone while Mother looked in the little mirror over the desk. She patted her hair and then touched her cheek. I wondered if she would tell Charles and Anna what happened to her face.

When my cousins came, we sometimes went to the creek, swung out over the water, and splashed in. That was especially fun on Sunday afternoons when the heat and humidity were so high that just breathing was an effort.

Today was sunny, but still spring-cool, and our cousins wanted to play a game of baseball. I liked to play ball, but Carrie thrived on it. She liked to imagine she was Billy Sunday, Iowa's most famous player. She was happy to play outfield, just like Billy, and that pleased the boy cousins who always chose the teams.

Usually we played to win, but today my heart was not in the game. I noticed my brothers and Carrie looked glum too. Finally, I went in the house for a plate of cookies and a jar of ginger ale that we had stored in the cellar.

As soon as I got in the kitchen door, I felt tension like the electricity in the air just before a lightning strike. The door to the living room was closed. Beyond it, Uncle Charles and Aunt Anna were both shouting. Shouting! I drew near the door and listened.

"Mary, you cannot divorce Vincent," Charles was saying.

The breath went out of me. Divorce! Was Mother planning to divorce Father?

Aunt Anna came to Mother's defense. "Charles, look at her. She can't stay with him."

"There's good reason the church is against divorce," Uncle Charles countered. "You marry for better or worse. Things get better if you wait it out."

"Charles, if she waits, she might not be alive to see things get better!"

Charles's voice dropped. Evenly he warned, "You will break Babi's heart." Babi was the nickname someone had given Grandmother Spirek. It was short for the Bohemian name for grandmother, Babicka. Even I knew that was an unfair thing for Charles to say. No one, especially my mother, wanted to hurt Babi. Mother was sobbing again.

The tightness in my stomach and chest had grown, making it hard to breathe. My hands trembled. I was shocked to hear the shouting. Shocked to hear my mother crying again. Shocked they were talking about divorce. My mind whirled. What to do? What to do? Should I tiptoe away and pretend I had not heard? Should I open the door and let them know I was there? I gripped one hand in the other to steady myself and gulped for air.

"Have confidence in your mother," Anna said to Charles. "Babi will understand and want Mary and the children to be safe." However, Charles was not ready to let it go.

"All of this happened because you married outside the church. You should have known no good would come of someone who wouldn't stand before God to be married."

Finally, Mother seemed to get her voice.

"That's not why we were married by the judge. 'Twas because we didn't want to wait for the banns to be read." She sounded defensive, yet did I detect a little smile in her voice?

Charles snorted. "Couldn't wait three weeks? Mary, that's ridiculous."

Anna spoke up again; this time her voice was calmer, but she would hear no more arguments. "That was all a long time ago. Let's not rehash the past. We must deal with today."

Mother spoke again. "We had a lot of good years. I wouldn't trade my life with Vincent."

Charles sputtered and was silent. When he finally spoke again, he sounded more like himself. "There now, Mary. Do not cry any more. We'll figure something out."

At that, I crept away from the door, willing my hands to quit shaking. Grabbing the plate of cookies from the table, I slipped out the kitchen door.

Someone had just made a home run, and there was a lot of happy screaming and yelling when I got to the backyard. But Carrie looked at my face and said, "Bessie, you're white as Mutt's fur. Don't you feel good?"

I just shook my head slowly and handed her the cookies.

"Hey, where's the ginger ale?" George asked.

"If you're thirsty, go get some water from the pump!" I replied testily and turned away. The game was over as far as I was concerned. I started for the creek. Carrie, Emma, Ella, and little Lottie looked at each other and fell into line behind me like a family of ducks walking single file. The boys ignored us and turned their attention to the plate of cookies. We cut through the trees and turned toward the creek.

The trees were just leafing out and did not offer us a dark dome as they did in summer, but the sun felt good in the chilly air. We sat down on the bank together, commencing our own private girls club. I stared as water rippled around a rock in the stream. The other girls must have sensed I had a lot to say because they waited silently.

In the background, I heard my brothers talking loudly with our cousins James and Frank. They had regrouped and were playing ball without us. I lifted my head slightly and let my eyes slide to the side to look at the other girls.

Carrie sat at the other end of the row, trying to be so grown-up. She had the quickest tongue in the neighborhood, but her smart remarks were a cover for her tender inside. Now she looked straight ahead at the stream, her jaw moving, as it did when she was think-ing hard.

Lottie, age five, sat next to Carrie, her hero. She even rumpled her skirt to look more like Carrie's untidy clothing. More than any-thing, little Lottie wanted to be part of the "big girls." I would rather not have such a child hear what I had to say, but I could hardly send her back to the house either.

Emma was sixteen and the most grown-up. I was surprised she still hung around with us younger girls. But then, maybe like me, she didn't quite belong with the children or the adults. She was almost a head taller than I was and at least fifty pounds heavier. She wore her dark hair up now, like a real woman. Her personality was placid, like a quiet inlet in the bubbling stream before us. I tried to put on Emma's peaceful nature now by taking a deep breath.

Ella was fourteen and the closest thing I had to a best friend, if sisters did not count. Her personality sparkled as brightly as her blonde hair. Ella always had kind words about others and funny stories about herself. I loved the way she threw her head back when she laughed. However, she could be serious too, and we often traded our deepest secrets. It was really to Ella that I spoke that day.

By the looks on their faces, my cousins had seen my anxieties. The events of the day were too fresh for me to hold inside anymore.

"In my head, I think any problems will go away," I began cheerfully. Carrie kicked a stone into the creek. "But my heart isn't so sure—"

"What are you talking about?" asked Ella, taking my hand.

"Spit it out, Bessie!" I could see Carrie's jaw working. A sure sign she was about to say something *I* would regret.

"Father is not living with us anymore," I said, trying to find words that would lessen the shock of what was happening in our family. "He was very angry at Mother and hit her. He left in the middle of the night." Yes, that was it. I would report the facts and let them speak for themselves. Most of the facts. I left out the part about his drinking.

Ella sucked in her breath. Lottie looked at Carrie and asked, "Your father hit your mother?" Emma reached over and grasped my hand, and I came undone like a loosely tied ribbon sliding out of my fine hair. Tears found paths down my face, but I braved on.

"You see, Father isn't the same since the accident. His back hurts so bad that he gets mad. And takes it out on us."

Ella seemed to struggle to understand. "He hit your mother?" I nodded my head, unable to speak. "Has he hit you?" I shook my head.

"He didn't hit Bessie, but he pushed her good and hard!" Carrie jumped in, eager to give her account. "He won't let her go to school any more. And he is mean to Joe. I think—"

"Carrie, stop!" I finally found my voice. "No, Father hasn't hit me and, really, I guess 'twas time for me to quit school and do more of the work around here."

Too late, I remembered how much Charles and Anna prized education. They not only let Emma finish eighth grade but also sent her to high school. She boarded in Fort Dodge during the week and only came home on weekends.

"Oh, Bessie, I'm sorry to hear that. I know how much you liked school. You're the only person I know who could have fun learning." This from Emma, who always behaved properly and probably never giggled in the classroom.

Suddenly I realized how different we were from our cousins, even though we all lived in Webster County and were part of the same family. Charles and Anna were the kind of parents I wanted. They were quick to sympathize and give a helping hand. In our family, love and kindness were doled out as rarely as holiday chocolates. Charles and Anna did not worry about every penny, where our parents were just getting by. They went to church and school, while we were becoming more and more cut off from others. My eyes locked with Carrie's. Was she having the same thoughts? I felt shame splash up from my heart and color my face, but Carrie stuck out her chin. What caused me shame made her defiant.

"I might as well tell it all," I said reluctantly. I seldom turned red, but I could feel my face heating up. "Things may change in our family forever. Father may never come home." Those were the facts—not nice, but neat.

Carrie gawked at me, a big question mark across her face. All five of us sat, clenching each other's hands. In the distance, we could faintly hear the boys shouting something about the ball. They were but distant echoes in the quiet as each girl sorted through her thoughts.

A long time passed before Emma whispered, "We shall always be like sisters. No matter what happens." At that moment, her words felt like a warm blanket on a cold day. I would not catch their irony for some time to come.

A moment later, Uncle Charles came thrashing through the trees behind us. As he neared, he began shouting that it was time to leave. We could hear the upset in his voice. Emma, Ella, and Lottie looked at each other in surprise and then scrambled up the bank.

Carrie and I got to the farmyard as Charles swung little Lottie onto the seat of the wagon next to Anna. The other kids all crawled into the back as he "hawed" the team into action. They wheeled around the driveway, raising a cloud of white dust as they turned onto the narrow road leading away from the farm.

Mother was nowhere in sight. Normally she would stand in the middle of the yard and wave until visitors were out of sight. I alone had heard the angry discussion between the adults. Certainly, that was why Mother failed to make her usual farewells.

Carrie and I clung to each other. George turned and led Joe toward the outhouse. Eddie looked afraid, as if he had just seen the *bogo*, or boogeyman. He reached for Bill's hand, but Bill shrugged him off and stood looking after the wagon.

"Makes you wonder what just happened in the house, doesn't it?" Carrie said. I walked over to Eddie and hugged him. He grabbed me around the waist and hung on tight.

I remembered when he was a baby and Mother would put him in my lap and let me rock him to sleep. Later, when he could walk, he would come up to me and lay his head on my lap. However, he was seven now, and he had not needed such comfort for a while.

I looked at the house and wondered about Mother's state. I did not wonder long; even from a distance you could hear her banging pots and pans around and throwing things.

5

We did not see Father for the next month, but buggy traffic was heavy on our road. Someone from the Spirek family stopped by every day. They would send us kids to weed the garden while the adults talked.

When the steamy Iowa summer set in, the number of visiting relatives dried up like a stream in the heat. Mother and George went to the fields every day, coming in at night grimy and exhausted. There was no doubt that without Father the farm work was falling behind.

Carrie and I cooked, kept the house, and watched the other boys. We learned how to make a pot of soup last for days. We could make biscuits in our sleep. We also used up the sausages hanging in the smokehouse. By mid-June, I did not know how we could keep on.

Then one day, Babi drove up the road in her little buggy. She came in the house carrying her satchel, put on Mother's apron, and took charge.

Was I glad to see her! I preferred being a helper and not having all the responsibility for my brothers, the house, and cooking. Babi not only began cooking; she took care of a pile of laundry that had built up. Along with helping us during the day, Babi held late-night discussions with Mother.

Babi and Mother carried their strength differently. Babi remained calm, while Mother stomped around, shouted, and sometimes threw things. My aunties said reverently that Babi's faith in

God sustained her, but I had overheard my uncles chuckle that she was tougher than a boiled owl.

I was in awe of Babi. She had left her parents behind when she came to America. She traveled across the ocean and the prairie with small children in tow. Why, Mother was only one year old when they left Bohemia. Many other women had done this, but none of the others was my own grandmother.

I loved visiting Babi, who moved to a two-story house in Fort Dodge after Děda Spirek died. She had a swing in the backyard, and the Des Moines River flowed nearby. My brothers liked to go watch the new Webster County Courthouse being built a few blocks away.

In contrast to Mother and Babi's iron strength, my aunts were soft and sweet. I was especially fond of Uncle Anton's wife, Annie, who taught me so much without raising her voice or becoming impatient. One day when I was four, Mother barked at me for being afraid to cross the railroad tracks on the way from Babi's house to the river. However, Aunt Annie took my hand and explained exactly how to look and listen for a train. Then she showed me how to lift my skirt up and step between the rails.

"See?" she said demonstrating how to do it. "Those are the rules for safe crossing. If you always follow them, you'll have no reason to fear." Annie also taught me that a little love and sympathy could raise you up like yeast-raising dough. It was her example I had followed on my eleventh birthday when I comforted Mother in the dark of night.

Babi's arrival that June day was a welcome surprise, but a bigger one happened a week later. One morning, I came downstairs to find Father sitting at the table. I stopped when I saw him there, his shoulders hunched and his hands folded in front of him.

Mother was at the cookstove, stirring some porridge to death. Father looked up at me with sad eyes. When he saw me, his face softened, and he winked. From when I was little, a wink from Father was like a secret code that said that everything would be fine. Warm water hit the ice around my heart and melted it. I stood there for a long moment staring at him, until Mother turned around and ordered me to go get the cows in for milking. A few minutes later, Father left.

That afternoon, the priest from Fort Dodge came to visit. Uncle Charles had brought him to the farm a few weeks earlier, and the adults sent me outside so I would not overhear their conversation. However, this day I was in the sewing room off the parlor stitching a hem when he arrived. With a curtain covering the door, they could not see me, but I could faintly see them and clearly hear them. I did not dare show myself and hoped they would not catch me eavesdropping, quiet as a little mouse.

Mother offered the priest the velvet-covered chair and she sat down on the couch.

"Mrs. Kloubec, I visited with Vincent, and I've come to plead his case," he said.

Mother immediately stood again. "Father, how can you come into my home and plead the case for that man? He nearly killed me. Is everyone against me?" she asked, touching the scar on her face.

"Mrs. Kloubec, I met with Vincent. He is sorry. He wants to come home and take his place as the head of the family. He's thought this all out, and we have discussed it."

"You make it sound like it's Vincent's decision," Mother responded. "I am the one who was abused and am afraid." *What a tough spot for Mother*, I thought. We really needed Father in so many ways. I wondered if she was both afraid he would come back and afraid he would not.

"Think, Mrs. Kloubec! You have a large family to support and a farm to work! How will you manage without your husband? And I can tell you he is very sorry for the things he's done."

Mother sat down and hung her head. "The past year has been grim," she confessed. "You don't know what it's been like here. Vincent is not himself. He's not sane," she emphasized.

I could hear the urgency in her voice as she tried to make the priest understand.

"He corners me or takes his anger out on Joe. Or the dog. It can be any one of us. I am afraid for my girls and my little boys. What might he do to them if he has a stick or a gun when he's out of his mind?" Her voice drifted, as though she were reliving a terrible moment.

The priest continued his plea. "But he assures me he can handle the pain now. Besides," he added, "most disagreements take two people. Perhaps you should consider how you've contributed to the problem."

So, I wondered, did the priest think Mother was to blame for their fights? Then I must be guilty too or Father wouldn't be so mean to me. However, he was also mean to my brothers and Mutt. We would need to change if Father came home. But how?

The priest had a solution for Joe's problems. "To help relieve some of the stress, Vincent wants to send Joseph to the Iowa Institute for Feeble-Minded Children. I commend him for this decision. Joseph will be in good hands there. He will receive treatment from educated people. Living among his own kind is the best way."

"Do you realize how much Vincent has been drinking?" Mother said as though she had not heard the priest's last words. I had heard them loud and clear and could not believe Father wanted to send Joe away and that the priest approved it.

Mother continued, "Do you realize that Vincent hangs around at the tavern?"

"Oh, Mrs. Kloubec, Mary, is there a man who doesn't have a drink once in a while to lose the cares of the day?"

"Yes," Mother said. "My father didn't drink, and most of my brothers will not touch alcohol."

"A pious group," said the priest. *Wasn't he supposed to be against drunkenness?* I wondered. The priest continued his hard line. "If you divorce Vincent, you will be in very poor standing with the church. Your family may disown you."

Mother was silent for a moment and then said brashly, "My family wouldn't disown me! As you well know, only half of them are still in the church. They will not let the church dictate their lives like that! Why, one reason they left Bohemia was for freedom of religion."

The priest went on, "Don't be so certain. Freedom of religion is not the same as freedom from God. We must all answer for our actions. The Holy Bible says God hates divorce. I'm not sure you or your relatives want to be on the wrong side on this."

Silence filled the room. I struggled to be quiet, holding my nose against a sneeze. Mother would surely break the commandment, "Thou shall not kill" if she found me behind the curtain.

When Mother failed to respond, the priest tried another avenue. This time his voice held sympathy. "Mary, your children need their father. You need a husband. How can you possibly provide for your family alone?"

Another pause. Then a sob broke the quiet. He had touched the heart of Mother's biggest concern, one that overwhelmed her every day as she scrambled to take care of the animals, plant the crops, keep the house, and keep us from financial ruin.

"Mary, I want you to come to the church on Saturday. Come to confession. It will be good for your soul. Then I will arrange for a meeting with Vincent and you. I'll be present to help with any difficulties."

"As you wish," Mother reluctantly agreed. I sat back, stunned. If Father came home, how could I ever be good enough so he wouldn't get angry at me? And how could I keep Eddie safe? And why was it a sin to send your husband off, but all right to send a child away?

The next Saturday, Mother hitched up her horse and buggy and drove to Fort Dodge. A week later, Father came home. 'Twas the last Sunday in June as we sat at the breakfast table. He walked in the kitchen door and said, "Can I get a cup of coffee?"

We all sat surprised and staring. Then Mother smiled and went to the cupboard. She brought out a plate and cup for him. Eddie jumped up and ran to him, putting his skinny arms around Father's waist. I had to blink tears away, thinking how much Eddie needed a father's love. Carrie grinned. George and Bill tried to keep any expression off their faces. Joe shouted, "Father back! Father back," and knocked his fork against the table.

Father patted Eddie on his head. Then he set his satchel down and took his place at the table.

"Have you said the Pater Noster?" he asked Mother.

"No. Maybe you will lead it?" she answered politely. And he did.

I do not know all the bargaining that had gone on between them to bring him back. I felt relief that we were a family again as well as fear that Mother had made the wrong decision.

6

July 1899

For all we had been through that year, the Fourth of July holiday turned out surprisingly normal. Father moved back home. My grandmother, Babi, moved back to Fort Dodge. My whole family looked forward to the big Spirek family picnic. We held it every year in the park along the Des Moines River.

This was a dress-up affair. Mother braided up my hair while it was still wet, and we all wore our best summer dresses. I wore the white dress with a blue sash that Babi and I had made on the sewing machine when she stayed with us.

As pretty as the dress was, it reminded me of why Babi stayed with us. Sometimes those thoughts brought the lump back to my stomach.

We arrived early and watched as each family's wagon, piled high with kids and food, rolled in for this once-a-year family gathering.

We cousins had so much fun running three-legged sack races and playing Red Rover. Of course, we spent a good amount of time catching up on each other's lives.

For the picnic, women covered the rough wooden tables in colorful cotton cloths and tended to the food—fried chicken, sliced ham, potato salad, garden-fresh radishes, peas, and lettuce. Every woman tried to outdo the rest with her best dessert. Rhubarb pies and cakes were at the top of the list, most of them made with fresh fruit and farm cream. However, my personal favorite was Juneberry pie. I always kept a close eye on those pies and got in line early to get a piece. It didn't matter at all that Juneberries turned my teeth purple.

On this day, I also kept an eye on Father. Would he fit in with my uncles when they obviously knew what he had done to their sister? Mother's bruises had healed, but her scar still showed in white contrast to her tanned skin. Still, I was not surprised when my uncles acted like nothing had happened.

The men always talked about the same things. First, they discussed the crops and livestock. Then they started on their clubs.

"The Catholic Bohemian Society is the best lodge in Fort Dodge!" one would say.

"If you haven't belonged to the Bohemian Men's Association, you'd probably think that!" another countered. When they quit trying to solicit lodge memberships, they began arguing over politics.

Eventually someone would bring up a story printed in the *Slova Amerik'y*, the Bohemian newspaper published in Cedar Rapids. Then talk turned to the old country. Our grandparents came to America almost forty years earlier as a young married couple. First they moved to Iowa City, where many Bohemians settled, but eventually they bought land farther west in Webster County.

The men liked to tell how no one could get ahead in the old country but here a man could succeed. Why, look, they all had their own land and livestock! In Bohemia, you were lucky to own a cow, let alone a piece of land. If they had stayed over there just a few more years, they would not have been able to escape.

As in every conversation they had, someone pointed out, "Bohemia was such a hard place. They did not even worry about moving to America in the middle of the Civil War. War was a way of life in Bohemia."

Their patriotism surely equaled that of the Founding Fathers when they met in Philadelphia that steamy summer of 1776. Now in 1899, these men were just a bunch of Iowa farmers, but the world belonged to them because they lived in a free society.

The atmosphere rang with patriotic tunes played by a band all decked out in blue uniforms with brass buttons. Of course they played the "Star Spangled Banner," but also a new song that was really pretty called "America the Beautiful."

After the western horizon turned orange and the stars came out, the fireworks started. My brothers and boy cousins shot off one too many firecrackers. The adults shooed them off to make noise elsewhere, with warnings not to blow off their fingers.

The rest of our family gathered near the river for the annual show. We sat close together, Father next to Mother, Joe next to her, and Carrie and I snug with happiness. It looked like things were going well between our parents. I looked up to see Ella smiling at me. She too saw this special moment, and my heart warmed to share it with her. Emma, on the other hand, gave me a funny little smile, as though she thought I had made too much about our family's problems.

Still, as days go, July 4, 1899, was my best ever in eleven years. Isn't that the way life goes? Within a month, I had hit both the lowest low and the highest high. Something about that gave me a strange peace. It set up in my mind that no matter how bad things went, something good might be around the corner. Where some people always look for the bottom to fall out, I began looking for the top to appear again.

Sadly, that Pollyanna outlook could not change what came next.

7

August 1899

That summer, Father and Mother tried to make us into a family again. Father's face was pale and his body stooped, but he did not drink anymore. Mother acted more cheerful and showed more patience than usual.

We began going to church on Sundays, all of us riding in the wagon, except George who rode his horse alongside us. Father surprised us by buying Carrie and me lacy three-cornered veils to wear in church. I could not remember him ever buying us something like that before. It touched my heart as much as when he would give me a wink and a smile.

Because most of our lives looked normal, I could not put my finger on why I had a feeling of impending doom. Sure, Mother still seemed a bit fearful and Father had a lot of pain, but their words and actions said everything was okay. I decided I just had the jitters.

Then one day when Mother, Carrie, and I were in the kitchen, Mother dropped the other shoe, so to speak. We were making pickles from the cucumbers and onions we had picked that morning. We sliced them up, scooped them into a gallon crock, and poured brine over the top. When we finished, we planned to cover the crock with a large plate and let it work in the cellar. This kind of pickle hardly ever made it through the fall, because the boys were always sneaking tastes.

Mother had something on her mind that day. She seemed a bit too jolly. I thought about a letter I had found a few days earlier, when I had walked out to the mailbox beside the road.

"Have you ever heard of the Iowa Institute for Feebleminded Children at Glenwood?" Mother asked as she slashed through a cucumber with her knife.

"We learned about it in fourth grade," I said, "when we studied Iowa state history."

"Now that Joe is thirteen, almost grown-up, wouldn't it be nice if he could go there?" Mother asked. We could see Joe outside in his fenced area, picking up clods of dirt and throwing them in the air. They landed all over him. Mutt was with him but sat far enough away to miss the shower of dirt.

"Land's sake! You can't send Joe away to live with strangers!" Carrie burst out. She understood the direction of the conversation right away. "He's our brother! He's your son!"

Carrie had fiercely defended Joe for years. None of the kids at school dared say anything about him or they would have to deal with Carrie. At home, she often cared for him, towing him behind her like a little tugboat maneuvering a ship.

"Carrie, I don't want to send Joe away," Mother responded, impatiently. "I love him too. We were so happy the day he was born. He was a pretty baby from the start." Mother purred and then frowned. "Then about the time he began walking, he had a terrible fit."

"But that is near Nebraska. 'Tis so far away we'll never see him!" Carrie cried.

"Carrie, comes a time when a family can't take care of their own as well as others can. Joe is almost man-sized. 'Tis hard for any of us to handle him when he has a fit," Mother explained.

"I can handle him! I'll take care of him!" Carrie said. I wish I had a picture of her at that moment, only nine years old and ready for a boxing match with Mother.

"Besides," Mother went on, ignoring the challenge, "without Joe here, life will settle down more." *Ah*, I thought, *that is the bottom line.* Father had been trying hard to be kind to Joe, but I swear that vein in his neck still popped out when Joe did something annoying.

Carrie stomped her foot, but before she could say anything more, Mother gave her a withering look. She had said too much. "Go to your room before I swat you! This isn't your decision."

Later that day when I went to the pasture to bring in the cows, I had some time to think. The grass had the dried-out look of late summer, but many kinds of prairie flowers still bloomed and the scent of sage filled the air. Insects droned steadily in the late after-noon heat. Summer surrounded me, but all I could think about was Joe.

In truth, Joe had fewer of the spells as he got older, but they were still severe. He actually seemed to get more childlike as he grew taller. Maybe the spells took something away from his mind. I do not know for sure.

He could be loud and unpredictable, and he was not welcome at many places any more. He could not go to school. He had had a spell at the general store in Moorland, so he no longer went to town with us. Our relatives didn't say as much, but we knew they were glad when he was left at home during visits. He even wore on Babi's nerves. She treated him like a wild calf let loose in her house. Every time he moved, she jumped up to ward off calamity.

Thus, Father and Mother left him home most of the time. That meant when the family went to town or went visiting, I was often stuck at home watching Joe. Since I no longer went to school, I had even fewer chances to get out. I vowed when I grew up, I would have lots of friends and go visiting every chance I got.

I tried to banish a thought that popped into my brain like a dandelion. If Joe left, I could go to town more often, and I would not have to take care of his every need. A picture of myself all dressed up and riding beside Father in the wagon floated through my head, but I pulled my guilty thoughts back with a jerk. "Bad sister!" I said aloud. I loved Joe. Certainly my parents did too. Turning over his care to complete strangers was out of the question.

8

September 1899

School started in mid-September when the summer farm work began to let up. Carrie, Eddie, and Bill trudged down the road each morning, swinging their books and lunch pails. Of course, I envied them. The whole Spirek family talked about the importance of education being the ticket to a better life. Now I would have to make do with only six years of schooling.

Still, I did not miss hearing the unkind remarks of other students. Our family had always put up with whispered remarks about Joe, but the past spring, it got worse. Word got around soon enough when Father moved out. They said Mother was an old battle-ax who drove Father to drink and then drove him out the door. Others snidely said Father was not able to handle his liquor.

Mother's retort was you knew who your friends were because they stuck up for you and believed the best about you, no matter how things looked. If someone always found the bad in your life, that person really was not your friend. I did not feel I had many friends over at the school.

The neighbors certainly had doubts about the Kloubec family all along. Now they probably discussed me because I had dropped out of school. I tried to think like Mother. If they wanted to believe the worst, so be it.

Carrie tended to take things into her own hands at school. One time she "accidentally" bumped one of the gossipers into a mud puddle. Another time she tripped a girl, and when she fell flat on her face, Carrie just looked surprised and said, "Oops!" So many accidents happened around Carrie that the other girls learned to leave her alone.

My brothers fared better, maybe because their boy classmates were less interested in gossip. Still, Bill and Eddie both got into some playground scraps when the other boys teased them about Joe or our parents.

George and Father worked outside most days, while Mother and I preserved food for winter. Joe spent time with us or in his fenced-in farm, as he had taken to calling it. He had put together some farming tools and always took his toy soldier along to help with the work.

Although things looked routine, the atmosphere on the farm was uneasy, like a truce called in a war. It felt like trouble could break out any moment. And one day it did. One September afternoon as I pulled clothes off the line and folded them into a basket, Mutt woofed once. I looked up to see Tader Smith riding up the driveway. Like other neighbors, he sometimes asked Father to repair a part for him, so I figured that was why he stopped by.

I waited while he got off his horse. With a smirk on his face, he looked me up and down as if I stood there in my underwear.

"Yer Father around?" he asked.

I nodded toward the house as I cracked a towel and began to fold it. Father liked to stretch out on the parlor floor, a place that comforted his back, in the middle of the workday. Tader Smith tied up his horse and went into the house. A few minutes later, he and Father came out and went to the barn.

It did not seem like the beginning of the end. The windmill creaked in the steady breeze. I could hear the faint sound of water running into the cattle tank, the buzz of fall insects, and the chirp of crickets. In the midst of that earthy peace with the sky blue to the horizon, Tader Smith shared a bottle with Father in the darkness of the barn.

The general store in Fort Dodge had a scale with a metal plate on each side. The weights on the scale measured items in fractions.

When I think of that September day, I picture the scale. All it took to change the delicate balance of our lives was one small temptation.

Mother said Tader Smith followed liquor, and trouble followed Tader Smith. It sure seemed true. His wife had a hard life and died young, and he could not seem to hold on to a job.

That day the delicate balance tipped, and Father's family, his farm, and his health began to slide off the scale. For a long time, I blamed Tader Smith, but now I know it really was Father's choice to go down that road.

In no time at all, the old tensions started back up as he once again leaned on alcohol to take away his pain. Mother did what she could to keep peace, but Father walked around like a threatening thunderstorm. We kids stayed away from him as much as possible, never knowing what kind of mood he would be in from one moment to the next.

Father began bringing his bottle into the house, where he would sit at the table after the evening meal. He started off in a happy mood, but it did not last. We made ourselves scarce to avoid his cruelty. He spoke in Bohemian when he drank, his words cutting like razors.

All fall, Mother had been quiet. She no longer clucked at us to get our chores done. She submitted to Father's outbursts with her head down. She usually played piano in the evening. Before, she played happy tunes, but now she played Bohemian dirges.

George, who was fifteen, often slipped out in the evening to be with his friends, so he missed much of the trouble. Father yelled at Bill for making too much noise, but otherwise left him alone.

Carrie went to our room and read the *Slova Amerik'y*, the *Fort Dodge Chronicle*, or the *Sears & Roebuck Catalog*. She enjoyed reading more than I did. I chalked that up to my weak eyes, but maybe she was just smarter. Sometimes she read our dictionary or borrowed books from the teacher. We only owned a handful of books, the most important being the family Bible. None of us read the Bible because the church said only the priests could understand it. We used it to record marriages, births, and deaths.

I often escaped to the sewing room off the parlor. The cozy little room had a large cupboard where we stored fabric and sewing notions, a square cutting table, and a rocker with a good oil lamp nearby.

Since Babi and I had made my dress that summer, I had begun using Mother's New Queen treadle sewing machine. I cut out several aprons and began stitching them on the machine. I sewed the ties inside out and used a safety pin to pull the fabric right side out. Once I sewed the ties on the apron, I finished them by embroidering colorful flowers on them. It was easy to lose myself in the sewing room when tension grew thick in the rest of the house.

Eddie was the one who took the brunt of Father's meanness. He always managed to wander into the kitchen at the wrong time.

"So what did you learn in school today?" Father would ask with a jovial air.

Eddie never seemed to expect Father to turn on him. "We had a spelling test."

"Well, how did you do?"

"I only had one wrong."

"You had one wrong? How can that be? How many days did you study those words?"

"A week, Father. I got all the rest right."

"A whole week and you couldn't spell the stupid word? How could you fail so badly? And which word did you misspell?"

"C-c-com-f-f-fort," Eddie stuttered.

"Comfort. Well that is an easy word. How could you miss it? Are you stupid? And why are you talking like that?" Father slammed his fist on the table, making the sugar bowl rattle, and Eddie jump. "Quit stuttering and talk like an American. I don't want to be ashamed of you."

All the while, Mother pounded out a dirge on the piano, drowning out the confrontation.

I knew a little of how Eddie felt. Father usually picked on me at mealtime for my eating habits.

"Bessie, why aren't you eating your chicken and potatoes?"

"I am, Father."

"You've been pushing your food around your plate since we started. *Now take a bite*," he would command.

I would put some food in my mouth, but I could hardly swallow it. Once it went down, it sat in my stomach for hours. I had not had an appetite for months.

These scenes happened repeatedly. One time Father jumped up from the table and came over to me. He put his hand on my neck and looked at my half-full plate, fury written on his face. I thought for sure he would begin pushing food down my throat, but then he got control of himself.

9

One bright October morning after the other kids went to school, Mother sent me out to the porch with a bushel of lima beans. I was supposed to pop them out of their shells, and then we'd dry them. In midwinter they tasted good cooked up with ham. Joe was working in his fenced-in area. He had dragged more tools over to the spot to help with his farming operation.

Before I got to working on the beans, I spied the hollyhocks growing along the side of the house. They must have been six feet tall by then, and the flowers were in a rainbow of pinks and blues, perfect for making hollyhock dolls. I took five round buds and five full flowers and started assembling them with toothpicks. Since I'd never had a real doll, apple and hollyhock dolls had to do. I knew how to make them any number of ways. These ladies were going to get dressed up and go to a dance.

When Mutt began to bark, I squinted into the sun. Shielding my eyes with my hand, I saw a wagon pulling into the driveway, with the drayman from Fort Dodge in the driver's seat and a woman sitting on the backseat. They came to a stop in front of the house as I stuffed the dolls inside the basket of beans.

The woman got down from the wagon and removed her duster, which she folded and laid on the wagon seat. She wore a gray suit with pearl buttons and a full skirt. Her hat was narrow-brimmed with a flock of feathers perched on the top. For a long moment, she looked over at Joe as he worked inside his fence. Then she sailed right up to me and asked to see Mr. or Mrs. Kloubec.

I just stared at her for a few seconds, remembering a letter I had found in Mother's apron pocket a week or two before. A nervous feeling flowed through my veins like hot water pouring through a lead pipe. I moved slowly to open the screen door. Mother was just coming down the stairs, and I motioned her to the door.

"Mrs. Kloubec? I'm Esther Goodhart from the Iowa Institute for Feeble-Minded Children. I've come for Joseph," said the woman.

My mouth dropped open. Mother swung the kitchen door wide so she could go into the house. I followed her inside as quietly as I could.

Miss Goodhart asked, "Did you receive our letter accepting Joseph into the school?"

Mother nodded. We probably both appeared a little slow ourselves to Miss Goodhart, as we were not saying much. Finally, Mother found her voice. "I don't much want to send him away," she said. "But he's getting too big for us to handle. I packed his things."

I stared in surprise when she motioned to Father's carpetbag, which stood near the stairs.

"I have some papers for you and Mr. Kloubec to sign."

"Bessie, run get your Father!" Mother said quietly. She stared at the woman, studying the character of Miss Goodhart, sizing up what kind of institution she represented. I backed through the door, tripped over the bushel basket, and did a fancy dance in order to stay upright. My pretty flower dolls spilled on the porch floor. Then a rush of nerves hit me, and I quickly trotted past the barn, out to the hay yard where Father and George worked.

"Father! Come quick! There is a woman here about Joe. Mother wants you to hurry."

He threw down his pitchfork and started for the house, mopping his face with a red hanky. I turned to George and said he better come too, and quickly. George nodded but went back to finish what he was doing. I was not going to waste time coaxing him to hurry. I ran back to the house and got to the step just as Father slammed past the door. I stopped on the porch and stood with my back to the wall between the screen door and the window where I could hear what was going on.

After introductions, Mother, Father, and Miss Goodhart sat down at the kitchen table. I could hear china rattling and figured Mother was taking out the good cups and saucers and putting a plate of coffee cake on the table also.

"I know how difficult this decision is," said Miss Goodhart. "But my own brother has been at the home for two years. He seems quite happy. In a way, the home is an experiment in how to treat people with handicaps. The home was founded on the principle of Christian charity. We seek to help those who will never be able to lead a normal life."

"The home is run by the state and not by a church," Mother pointed out.

"Yes. The state funds and runs the home, but the town's people are involved. Local churches sponsor birthday parties for the residents each month and have lovely Christmas parties for them. Civic clubs come in to play music for the people and play games with them. It has all gone much better than anyone dreamed. We have over eight hundred residents now."

She painted such a good picture that I envied Joe. Imagine, having a birthday party!

"We were surprised to get your letter saying you'd pick Joe up. We thought we'd take him to the home and then stay a few days," Father said.

"We prefer to not have families drop off the children. We also discourage families from coming to visit," Miss Goodhart explained. Suddenly the birthday parties didn't sound so good to me. No matter how good things sounded, Joe was still being sent to an institution.

"Oh," said Mother. A chair scraped as she stood up suddenly. "I don't know if I can do this. He is going to miss us and wonder why we sent him off. Won't you make an exception? I want to visit him in a few weeks. Surely, you allow for some family visits?"

"Mrs. Kloubec, it's our experience that a clean break with family is the best. Families do not like to hear this, but the children do not remember you. They live in the present, and they forget their families. If you come to see them, it stirs them up again."

"How much is this going to cost us?" asked Father.

"Once Joe is at the home, the state will take over his care. We'd like for you to pay for his train ticket and travel expenses."

"Well, the price is right," said Father.

"Here is a picture of the home. As you can see, we have beautiful brick buildings. We have 160 acres of farm land!" Miss Goodhart said enthusiastically. After a pause, she added, "There is one other thing. You both must sign papers giving up your rights to Joe. In effect, the state of Iowa will become his guardian."

"Where do I sign?" Father asked.

"Vincent! Are you sure this is the right thing to do?" Mother asked. Her voice sounded strange, as if she had a radish stuck in her throat.

"Mary, we have to do this. There is no other way."

"There is another way," Mother said evenly. "We've done right well with him, and we still can."

Mother sounded confused. She must have agreed to the idea in the beginning, but now she had doubts. Maybe she really did not know whether this was the right thing to do. Again, I realized that grown-ups are sometimes as confused as kids as they feel their way through life.

"I can give you a few moments to discuss this," said Miss Goodhart, "but that's all. My train leaves at noon, and I plan to be on it, with or without Joseph. We have only one opening, and we don't expect to have more space for some time."

"There's nothing to discuss." Father must have gotten up and gone to the drawer where we kept the pen and ink. All was quiet except for the faint sound of his pen scratching across paper.

"Very good," said Miss Goodhart. "We'll send you a letter in a week or two to report on Joseph's adjustment to the home. After that, there will be periodic reports. Now, may I meet the young man?"

"Bessie, go get Joe," Mother called. She had known all along that I was eavesdropping on the porch. I walked slowly down the steps and over to the fence. My stomach churned as if I would throw up any moment.

"Come on, Joe, there's someone here to meet you." We headed for the house, but out of the corner of my eye, I saw Joe's little soldier propped up in the dirt, as if he had been supervising the work. I scooped him up and stuffed him in Joe's pocket. The little soldier might be his only friend at his new home.

Mother ushered Joe up to Miss Goodhart and introduced him. Joe stood as tall as she. He looked her square in the eye. She smiled at him and spoke to him as if he were grown-up.

"Joseph, I'm glad to meet you," said Miss Goodhart. "Your parents told me so much about you. I feel like I know you already. I just stopped here on my train trip from Chicago to Omaha."

"Train?" Joe asked. He always ran to see the trains that rumbled on the tracks near Babi's house, but he had never had a train ride.

"Yes. It is quite something. The train chugs along, and you can watch the farms go by. Dark smoke comes from the engine. And the seats are made of green velvet."

"Smoke!" said Joe, remembering smoke coming from an engine he had seen. "Joe like trains!"

Miss Goodhart's face softened, and her eyes lit up. "Would you like to go on a train ride with me? We'll go to a place that has a big farm."

"Joe like farm," he responded. Miss Goodhart was saying all the right things to entice him. Joe looked at Mother. Her eyes glistened with tears, but she nodded to him. I heard Father weasel out the door. He was not even going to say good-bye!

"Joe go!"

Both women sighed in relief that he was willing to go with Miss Goodhart. I could not believe the trickery they were using.

How could Mother not tell Joe that he was going away forever? How could Father sneak out the door?

Suddenly I decided someone needed to tell Joe what was happening, but before I could say a word, Mother grabbed my arm and squeezed it hard. Her eyes flashed with warning. "Bessie," she said evenly, a livid look in her eyes, "Joe's suit is hanging in the sewing room. Please take him in there and help him get dressed."

"Joe, you can go with Miss Goodhart on the train!" Mother said, a false note in her cheerful voice. "Now let Bessie help you put on your good suit!"

I led Joe out of the room. I did not dare tell him the truth or punishment would surely be swift. However, I did whisper to him repeatedly, "I love you. Carrie loves you, George loves you, Eddie loves you, and Bill loves you."

I could not bear to say Mother and Father loved him. How could love send a child off with a complete stranger to an unknown future? When we walked outside, George stood there, his eyes big.

"Joe is going on a train trip to Glenwood with Miss Goodhart," Mother explained to George, her eyes holding the same warning she had given me. George shrugged and gave Joe a brotherly clap on the back. Mother held Joe close and then let him climb up the wagon by himself. She held her chin high, though I thought I saw a tremor there.

Father was nowhere to be seen.

Just like that, Joe was gone, sitting on the backseat of the dray, waving happily to Mother, George, and me.

I went directly upstairs after that and threw myself across the bed. Mother called a couple of times. She wanted me to do the lima beans, but I ignored her. How could she have the heart to go about her day as if nothing happened?

To me, sending Joe away was worse than a funeral. At least when Grandfather Spirek died you could go visit his grave in Graceland Cemetery. But for the rest of my life I would wonder what really happened to Joe. Was he still alive? How was he doing? What more should I have done for him?

I soaked three hankies with my tears before falling asleep that day.

A ball bouncing rhythmically against the wall finally woke me. *Whap. Whap. Whap. Whap.* Carrie was sitting on the floor, her back to the closed door of our room. She must have been tossing the little ball for a long time. Her jaw was clenched, and her mouth turned down.

"Carrie, come here," I whispered. She crawled up on the bed with me. Her nine-year-old chin began to quiver, and then she started to cry. We cried together, holding each other tight until the sun began to lower in the late afternoon.

Eventually I went downstairs, but Carrie stayed in our room the rest of the day, not even going down for supper that night. Sometimes she would throw the ball again, and I could hear it bounce across the floor above my head. Sometimes she whacked the pillow against the bed until I wondered if pillow feathers were flying all over our room.

Still, Carrie was not the one I worried about. I went to find Eddie.

I looked through the house and then the barn. Finally, I wandered down to the creek. Although the sun had set, George and Bill were still fishing in their usual spot. In the semidarkness, they did not see me as I moved past them through the trees to my special place. I knew Eddie sometimes went there too. Sure enough, he was on the bank, all hunched up, his little jacket closed tight against the chill of early evening.

"Eddie, come back to the house, 'tis getting dark out." I squatted down next to him, noting that he had gone back to the old habit of sucking his thumb.

"I met the lady who took Joe away," I said.

"You did?" Eddie asked in a muffled voice from behind his sleeve. "Was she mean?"

I thought a moment. "Not at all," I said. "She had a nice smile, and she treated Joe fine."

"Sure, while she was with you."

"She told all about the home and how 'twas made special for kids like Joe. They want to make Joe's life better. Maybe they will find a way to cure his fits. 'Tis a big, new red-brick building, and there are other kids like Joe."

"Are you saying it's a good thing?"

I had to think on that. I was brokenhearted about Joe going away and fearful of what might happen to him. And I was really, really mad at Mother and Father for sending him away.

Still…what if the home really was a better place for Joe? Suddenly the truth hit me. I had only been looking at the dark side of things again instead of seeing the possibility of good happening.

"Eddie!" I said. "Maybe this *is* the best way."

My voice held surprise as the truth dawned on me. It reminded me of when I learned to read and the alphabet began to make sense. I could sound out the words in my primer! That day I ran and skipped all the way home from school, filled with joy over the discovery.

I felt that way now as I saw both the gloomy underside of this tragedy and the other side that shone with the light of possibility. I gave Eddie a great big hug and pulled him up.

"Yes. It really is going to be all right!" I exclaimed. Eddie looked at me closely and saw I meant it. Then he relaxed in my arms.

"Come on, I think there's some bread and jelly waiting for us in the kitchen!" I said, pulling him toward the house.

Once in the light and warmth of the kitchen, I grabbed Mother and gave her a big hug.

"I know sending Joe away wasn't easy," I confessed. "I'm sorry if I made it any harder."

Mother hugged me back, and I swear I heard a sob trying to get out of her throat. I smiled at her, she smiled at me, and we both grabbed Eddie and brought him into the circle.

"'Tis going to be okay," Mother whispered. "Everything is going to be okay."

And it might have been, if sending Joe away had helped Father quit drinking.

10

November 1899

By November, the harvest was in, and we had filled the cellar with food preserved for winter.

My burlap bag of dried lima beans hung from the low ceiling beams in the cellar, next to bags of onions. Jars of peas, beans, and corn competed for space on the shelves with canned peaches, pears, and pickles. Squash and pumpkins lined one whole wall, and we toted potatoes down the steps and filled the bin in the corner. Twenty-gallon crocks held carrots and sauerkraut. It took us one full day to shred the cabbage for sauerkraut, but it sure was nice to get a scoop full to add to a winter meal. We were lucky that our cellar was right under the house, so we could reach our goods without going outside. All those delicious foods would make the long winter months easier.

I liked fall. It warmed me to see the shelves of preserved food, to add quilts to the beds, and to watch the world go dormant. I was still young enough to look forward to a howling snowstorm as much as the first fluffy white snowfall.

However, it made me shiver to think about the day Tader Smith had come over with his bottle. That day, our lives began a sad slide, like a cutting board full of sliced potatoes pushed into boiling water. Nevertheless, we kept up appearances until the middle of November.

Each year after harvest and before winter set in, the Spireks liked to lay up a supply of meat. This year, Anton and Annie, Charles and

Anna, Babi, and an assortment of young cousins came to our place to do the butchering.

Usually each family got a hog and shared a beef amongst them. The men also cured hams and mixed sausage. The women stayed indoors preparing sultz, a traditional food from the old country that we stored and served cold at our Christmas feasts. The scent of simmering spices filled the house. Land's sake, I loved the pumpkin pies this time of year as well as the cakes made with black walnuts we had picked and cracked. Even with my stomach tied in knots, I could poke down a whole piece of black walnut cake.

While some of the women worked in the kitchen, others set up the rug-making equipment in the parlor. All year long, we saved old clothes and tore them into strips to make rugs. Wheel rugs were the most fun to make because they did not take too long. One of my favorite parts was picking the cloth to use. You can end up with all colors of rugs. They are washable, and they feel good under your feet when you crawl out of bed in the morning.

We tied strips of cloth around the spokes of the wheel. Once we had tied them all the way around, we wove other strips through. Then we tied off the ends, leaving a little fringe. We usually finished a couple of new rugs by the end of the day.

There was always plenty of women's laughter on butchering day. Of course, not being grown-up but not being a child, it was my place to watch the little kids, Lottie, Rose, and David. I did not mind watching them, but it made me aware again that I was old enough to quit school and work but still not one of the women.

No one mentioned Joe. Missing him made my stomach churn, as much as did Father's anger. Still, I hoped Joe was in a better place. We had received a letter saying he had had a safe journey and was adjusting to his new home. He shared a room with other boys his age and still had his wooden soldier. There was a photo of him standing with Father's satchel in front of a tall brick building with a windmill in the background. I put it in my photo album.

My feelings about Joe remained mixed. I was relieved not to be responsible for him anymore but worried that God would punish me for such bad thoughts.

At the gathering, the other women told stories and laughed, but Mother remained silent. She nodded and smiled at the right times, but clearly her mind was elsewhere. The old tensions with Father had increased day by day, and I wondered what Mother would do about it. I also wondered if the Spirek family even knew what was happening to us.

The chatter in the house had grown to its afternoon peak when I suddenly felt a draft and looked up. My cousin James stood with the door wide open, holding a gun. Father's gun. The room grew silent. He marched over to Mother and pushed the gun at her, shouting, "My father said to give this to you. He said hide it quick."

Horrified, Mother and Babi stared into each other's eyes for several seconds. Babi seemed to turn pale. Then Mother took the gun and whisked it into the sewing room. I guessed by the sounds from in there that she put it in the sewing room cupboard.

Then she stalked out, more like the Mother I used to know than the meek shadow of a woman she had become. She quickly grabbed her shawl and swished out the door, slamming it behind her.

James started to rush out after her, but Aunt Anna grabbed him by the collar and pulled him back. James was about my age, and I vaguely wondered if he felt like me, caught between childhood and adulthood.

A shocked silence overpowered the room. As the minutes ticked by, we all stood like statues and stared at the door, straining to hear something from outside. I wanted to scream and run after Mother, but I could not even move my big toe. Why had Uncle Charles sent James in with Father's gun? Was Father all right? Was Mother all right? And George was out there with the men! *Dear God, protect them*, I prayed silently.

We stood straining to hear any sound. Finally, when the stillness was unbearable for another second, Aunt Anna took a breath and asked James what happened. He just started to speak when the sound of feet bounding up the porch step made us turn to stare at the door again. I fully expected Mother to come through the door, but instead Bill burst in, followed by Eddie and Carrie. They had arrived home from school in the midst of the crisis.

"What's going on?" Bill asked, excitement spilling out. "There are all kinds of noises coming from the shop. It scared us!" Eddie looked like a frightened puppy, and so did Carrie for that matter.

Their arrival seemed to help James find his voice, and he looked at Eddie when he spoke. "Your Father is plum crazy!" James said loudly, causing Eddie to shrink back. "Uncle Anton and my father had to wrestle him down! Father gave me your father's gun and told me to bring it in the house and give it to Aunt Mary before he shot someone."

Suddenly the whole room was abuzz with the news, but I only heard fragments of conversation. "Knew he was dangerous…" "Thought he was all straightened out…" "Bet he's been tipping the bottle again…"

The room seemed to swirl around me, and then Aunt Annie grabbed my shoulders, saying, "Come, Bessie, sit over here," she said as she led me to a kitchen chair. I tried to take a deep breath, but I could not seem to get enough air. Aunt Annie gave a look to the other women, as if to say, "Not in front of the children!"

Aunt Anna clamped her hand over James's mouth then, but the picture of what was going on in the shop was clear. The tightness in my stomach, the lack of air…Just when I thought I for sure was going to faint, Carrie and Eddie both came over and put their arms around me. Somehow their warmth poured strength into me, and I got a breath and then another.

I cannot say I ever cried very much and never in front of others, but that day I could not help it. Tears poured out of my eyes like water over a dam. I just cried and cried, until finally Aunt Annie and Carrie took me to our room. I shivered so hard my teeth chattered, so they tucked our biggest quilt around me. Aunt Annie sat next to me, her blue dress neatly folded around her, while Carrie crawled on the bed and sat stroking my hair.

"I just can't seem to s-s-stop crying," I said apologetically.

"'Tis all right," said Aunt Annie, her voice soft and soothing. "Cry all you want, Bessie. You're always so brave, but even very brave people sometimes cry." She looked up, as if she was seeing something in the distance, and murmured, "Dear one, you are only eleven years old. You cannot carry everything on your shoulders."

"Yes, Bessie, you're always the one who takes care of all of us, even Mother," Carrie said. For some reason that made me cry harder. Then Carrie quietly told Aunt Annie of the night I had comforted Mother, the night of my birthday.

"I-I thought you slept through all of that, Carrie," I said when she had finished.

"Well, I heard, but I was in such a deep sleep, I couldn't get myself to wake up," Carrie explained. "I thought 'twas a nightmare until I went downstairs in the morning."

We talked for a while longer before I drifted off, more relaxed than I had been in a long time and unaware of the events taking place elsewhere on the farm.

When I woke up, it was dark out, and I heard the sound of horse gear jingling and the grinding of wagon wheels. I hardly felt like moving, but I got out of bed anyway and wandered downstairs. Mother was scrubbing pans, and my brothers and Carrie sat at the table eating some beef and barley soup.

"Oh, Bessie," she said, "are you feeling better?" Her eyes inspected me. "Do you want something to eat?"

I sat down, planning to say something perky, but found I had no energy to speak. Someone passed the milk pitcher and put a bowl of soup in front of me. I was surprised to find I had an appetite.

"Uncle Anton and Aunt Annie just left." Carrie was the official newsperson. "Babi went back with them. They waited until everything got calmed down." I could see her shoulders lift in importance when Mother did not stop her oration.

"Charles and Anna took Father to Fort Dodge," Carrie continued. "They put him in the wagon, and Aunt Anna drove. Little Lottie sat scrunched next to her. Uncle Charles and James sat in the back with Father. They probably took him to jail!"

Mother turned from where she worked at the sink and gave Carrie the eye. Carrie looked down at her soup bowl. Then she looked up at me with her chin out. "I'm glad. I am glad they took him away. He could kill someone!"

"Carrie! That is enough. Go to your room!" Mother commanded. She slammed the dishtowel down, upsetting a stack of pans that began tumbling to the floor.

Clank! Clank! Ding! Crash! Clank! Lids rolled off under the table and into the corner like military wagons in a war. Mother stomped her foot and kicked one of the pans in her frustration. It clanked across the floor and rolled to a stop near the door. Carrie slid off her chair and slowly backed out of the room. Her eyes were big as lanterns, but she would not take back what she said.

"'Tis true!" Carrie shouted. "I'm glad he's gone." She turned and stomped up the stairs.

Mother's shoulders squared as she stared after her younger daughter, hands on hips. I looked at my impatient mother, pans all around her feet. A giggle escaped me. I laughed, quietly at first and then aloud, my shoulders shaking. I could not quit laughing. My brothers tried to stay composed, but my laughter infected them.

"Children! That is enough! This isn't funny!" Mother said just as another pan fell to the floor. That made us laugh all the harder. Then Carrie came out of the shadows, laughing also. Before long, Mother started smirking. She covered her mouth, but a laugh escaped anyway.

When I finally got my breath, I tried to explain my inexcusable behavior. My voice was high, and I could hardly speak. Tears ran down my face, but they were happy tears. "I know there isn't anything funny, but…but…Mother, you look so funny with those pans flying everywhere. You have not slammed things around for so long. Somehow 'tis comforting to have you back to normal."

I suddenly realized I had never feared Mother's stern ways or her impatience. She delivered no more than a scolding or a swat, whereas Father's anger menaced in some darker way. I took a deep breath, the first in a long time, feeling light and free, even though I did not know whether Father would come home or not. There wasn't one thing I could do about it, and the weight of the world was off my thin shoulders.

11

December 1899

December came with its early sunsets and cloudy days. I was in the dark too about what was happening to our family. Mother took a few trips to Fort Dodge, and Uncle Charles and Uncle Anton came out to visit her one day. This time, I could not eavesdrop because Mother made me ride to Callender with George for supplies.

Finally, Father came to the farm one morning with a man I did not know. I was glad to see Father was not sitting in jail, although the stern man seemed more like a guard than a friend. Father looked the same, but maybe a little more bent over and sad.

He brought in a trunk from the shop where it was stored. Then he gathered his clothes, some papers, tools, and a few other personal items and layered them in the trunk. Mother hovered nearby, complaining if he took anything that she needed to run the farm.

"Good grief, Mary," he finally said. "Do you want me to leave without even a hat? My pater brought some of these tools over from Bohemia. They won't do you any good, but they might help me make a living."

That was just before Christmas.

I have to say that 1899 was the saddest Christmas ever. I hate to admit it, but I did not help matters. Instead of trying to make things better for my family, I just sulked around feeling sorry for myself.

I had started out to make aprons for all my girl cousins but had not finished them. In the end, it had not mattered anyway because instead of visiting family, exchanging gifts, and singing "Silent Night," we sat in our silent house.

The whole of Christmas week was stormy, and we did not see the sun. When the wind first picked up and big goose feather snowflakes began swirling around, Mother and George had strung a rope from the house to the barn. When it was time to do chores, we followed the rope out. We always went in twos. There were all kinds of dark stories about people getting lost in snowstorms on the prairie. Even the cows and chickens were not producing much, so we had just enough eggs and milk to get by. We had to save up cream for quite a while to make butter.

I lay on my bed feeling oh so sad, as my mind drifted back to the wonderful Christmas we had the year before. Early on that Christmas morning, Mother had braided up my hair while it was wet. When it dried, I took out the braids and let the curls fall around my shoulders. I felt beautiful! But poor Carrie. Her hair had no natural wave, so mother used the curling iron on her and burned her ear.

The whole Spirek family had gathered at Anton and Annie's for Christmas 1898. They had a big house, and so many people came they just about had to stack the guests like cord wood. Wagons and buggies were parked all over the yard. The older boys led the horses into the giant barn and fed them. As people arrived, we forgot English and called out greetings of "*Vesela Vanoce!*" or Merry Christmas in Bohemian. (We pronounced it Veh-sell-ua Von-oats-uh.)

They had a beautiful Christmas tree decorated with red bows and popcorn. Annie set up a buffet, and everyone brought traditional Bohemian foods. You could count on having a big ham, dumplings, sultz, and poppy seed candy. Babi usually baked all Christmas Eve day, making hundreds of cheese, prune, and apricot kolaches. My family always brought a big roaster of fried chicken, a cast-iron pot filled with hot potato salad, and our specialty, jars of pickled watermelon and beets.

Someone played a fiddle in the drawing room, and people sang and laughed. I learned to dance at the family Christmas parties! We mostly did the polka, a Bohemian dance, and the schottische. People said I was light on my feet. Dancing made me feel so happy, I'd let out a "yahoo!" once in a while. At the same time, excited shouts signaled who was winning at a card game in another room. Children ran through the house like a train, upstairs and down. Women clustered in the kitchen, catching up on the family gossip.

That day, in the midst of all the happy chaos, there was a crash, the tinkling of broken glass, and a loud thud. Everyone stopped in midsentence, and the accordion hit a discordant note. It got so still that no whispered secret could have survived. The sound of thrashing and grunting began in the dining room. I nervously put my hand to my throat, realizing Joe was having a spell.

Sure enough, he had stumbled against a little shelf that held Annie's prized vase and figurine, brought to America by her parents. After traveling all that way, by ship, train, and covered wagon, the fragile pieces had now done a death dance in the air before crashing to the hard floor. I pushed my way through the crowd and stood gawking at my brother like the others. Joe writhed on the dining room floor amid the broken ruins. His eyes had rolled back in his head, and his body jerked. He was wet with sweat.

Mother acted quickly, fetching a wooden spoon from the kitchen. She knelt over him and pushed the spoon between his teeth so he would not swallow his tongue. Father and George arrived and struggled to hold him down, so his thrashing did not wreck the whole dining room.

The spell ended as quickly as it began. In the sudden silence, I was red-faced with embarrassment as I knelt to pick up the broken pieces of glass.

"Just old pieces of glass," Annie murmured, stringing her flustered thoughts along a clothesline of nerves. "Best to get rid of things from the past. Will Joe be all right? How can I help him? Someone get the broom and dustpan. Just old pieces of glass..."

The women began sending their children off to mind their own business, and the men drifted back to their card game. One of the fiddlers began playing softly again.

As for our family, each member went into action. George barreled outside to hitch up our team of horses, while I swept up broken glass. The little boys found our coats among the others heaped on a bed. Carrie gathered up our now empty roaster and other dishes. Mother apologized repeatedly to Anton, Annie, and the rest of the family, more flustered than I'd ever seen her. Finally, Father dressed Joe in his coat and, with Anton's help, carried his lanky body to the wagon.

Those were my happy and sad memories of Christmas 1898, but now this year would be remembered for the sound of a bitter wind rattling the windows. And why not? I mourned for the way things used to be, and not just Christmas. I sadly remembered Father and Mother dancing around the kitchen, so glad to own this land. Father telling joke after joke and my uncles laughing so hard they had to wipe their eyes. Joe charming us with his joy in being a "farmer."

Big questions entered my mind. If my parents could have foreseen the future, would they have bought this land? What could they have done to prevent this outcome? And what about me? How could I ever make any kind of decision, knowing that the sweet parts of life could turn out so bitterly?

The house seemed unusually dark for midday. The lamp offered only a small circle of light in the gloom. I stayed shrouded in the sewing room, away from the rest of the family, listening to Carrie chattering in the kitchen about the new century dawning in a few days. She expected exciting things to happen in the 1900s.

My thoughts were not as big as Carrie's. All I wanted was a normal life where no one shouted or drank too much. Where I didn't need to tell lies to cover awful truths. Where brothers were not locked away in institutions. A life where fathers did not come by the house to collect their few belongings.

12

January 1900

Jack Frost had painted the bedroom window like finely etched Bohemian glass. I ran my fingers over the translucent masterpiece and then began scraping off the frost with my fingernail so we could see outside. Carrie had dragged the quilt off the bed, wrapped it around herself, and looked out the window with awe.

This was our first look at January 1, 1900—a new year and a new century! When I had peeled off enough frost so we could both see through the window, the scene before us was prettier than a Currier and Ives plate. A blanket of snow sparkled like thousands of diamonds across the prairie. The same brilliant sun that exposed the diamonds paled the sky to the color of white linen colored by a drop of bluing.

"Nice to see the sun!" Carrie exclaimed.

I was quiet for a while before answering her. Finally, I asked, "Do you think 'tis a sign, like the rainbow God sent after the great flood? A promise that this year will be better than the last? How could a century start out so beautiful and not be good?"

"Well, things will have to be better than last year. A new century has to mean big changes," said Carrie, a nine-year-old expert on current events. "I think Australia will become a nation. We will finally get a national baseball league together. And you know those horseless carriages? Wouldn't it be grand to have one of those?"

We moved from the window reluctantly, each with our own thoughts of the future. The image of the sparkling snow stayed with me, and I said a little prayer, "Let it be a happy sign from above."

I decided to believe things were going to get better. It was a little like launching out to skate on the creek when you were not quite sure the ice was thick enough to hold you, but you try it anyway.

Then, as if to confirm my hope, we heard sleigh bells outside. I peeked out the window, and my heart skipped a beat. A fancy Austrian bobsled had pulled right up to the house. Uncle Anton and Aunt Annie sat on the front seat. Elizabeth and Adam, born on Christmas Day seven years ago, and Rose and David crowded onto the backseat, tucked under big warm robes.

I was so glad to see them, we all were. We flew to the door and began shouting "Vesela Vanoce!" They brought gifts for everyone and a basket of baked Christmas goodies. Mother put on the coffee and brought out the sultz. I went to the basement, got a pitcher of milk, and poured it into a pot to make hot chocolate for the kids. Annie pulled a loaf of fresh bread from the basket, and we had a feast.

Afterward, Aunt Annie opened her satchel and handed out gifts for each of us. We had not had any gifts on Christmas. I held the one she gave me for a long time. When I finally opened it, I found a round wicker basket. Aunt Annie was smiling at me.

"I hear you've become quite the seamstress. I thought you needed a special place to put your sewing notions," she explained.

Annie's thoughtfulness once again touched me to the core. I hugged her tight and whispered, "I'll keep it forever." Then I ran into the sewing room and came back with the one apron I had finished. It was of red-checked gingham. I had embroidered little blue and white flowers across the bottom. Now, I shyly presented it to Aunt Annie.

She picked it up and examined the stitches closely. "This is very well made, Bessie. You don't know how much I was wishing for a new apron. Thank you!" Mother seemed surprised by Aunt Annie's kind words. Mother had already pointed out every flawed stitch of my clumsy project.

They had gifts for everyone: a book for Carrie; a shiny new sled for the boys to share; and for Mother, a nice-smelling English lilac talc.

Afterward the boys went outside to play, and we girls went into the sewing room, which was cozy and warm. I wanted to put my thimble and some needles in my new little basket. The adults visited in the kitchen with the door closed. I did not know what they talked about, but I could guess.

January was typically cold and bright. The happy glow of that New Year's Day lasted for days. George took the shotgun and went looking for game on the better days. When he found a covey of pheasants, he usually managed to get a couple. George cleaned them, and Mother draped them with bacon, poured cream over the top, and roasted them. He also got prairie chickens and an occasional rabbit. They were a tasty break from the sausage, beans, and bread that often made up our weekday meals. We kept the hams and salted beef for Sundays or special occasions.

I cherished moments of happiness in the dead of winter. As often as possible, we played outside, pushing through the door with the energy of a train locomotive. The boys took the sled to the creek bank to see how far it would go on ice. We also skated on part of the creek where the ice was smooth. Of course, we did not have skates, but we had fun sliding around. Because there was plenty of snow, we began building snowmen and had a whole family set up behind the house.

One day George pulled me on the sled all the way to the schoolhouse. I will never forget the clear sky. We could see our breath and hear the crunch of the snow. Feeling happy, I smiled to myself, puzzled over how that could be when so many bad things had happened and the future was unknown.

Snowball fights were one of our favorite winter activities. We had been doing them for years. Usually the boys teamed up boys against the girls, and we would set up snow battlements and shoot snowballs at each other. Hidden behind snowbanks, we would sneak around and try to steal each other's snowballs, although Mutt often gave us away. Being outside in the snow, running, screaming and laughing, was probably the most I ever let go and felt free.

Then on January 19, after the other kids left for school, Mother surprised me by saying we were making a trip into Fort Dodge. She hurried me to get warmly dressed, saying that George was to stay home and mind the farm.

We rode horseback into Fort Dodge, letting the horses have their reign. They seemed pleased to be free as they clopped through snowdrifts that would stop a buggy first thing. I hadn't ridden a horse for a while, so it took a mile or so to get used to the sway and squeak of the saddle. The air was warmer, and the sun shown bright, like my mood the last few weeks. But as we rode through the pretty winter scene, I felt a dark cloud come over me as thoughts of Father passed through my mind.

He had planned to make a sleigh for us to replace the stoneboat he rigged up to make short trips to Moorland, three miles away. It was too big and awkward to go all the way to Fort Dodge. Most times, he or George rode horseback into town for the few supplies we needed. I missed Father. He had worked so hard on this farm, trying to make life better for us.

Life could be so unfair, I thought. The Spirek uncles often talked of how hard work brought prosperity. Then they looked down when they realized Father was there with them. They knew Father's hard work had not brought prosperity yet. I guess it is easier to bake a batch of cookies if someone else has already mixed up the dough. Money had passed down to my uncles and even to Mother. However, no one had given Father a dollar to get started. You might say he was making his cookies from scratch, while everyone else was already baking theirs. Now he had left behind the results of all his hard work.

I looked up and sighed. The land was so flat that I could see Fort Dodge in the distance. The trees along the Des Moines River formed a gray border, with smoke rising above it. I had not been away from the farm for weeks, so I tried to shake the dark cloud.

"Mother, why are we going into Fort Dodge?"

"I thought you'd like to visit your Babi, while I take care of some business."

"Are you going to see the banker?"

"No, I have business at the courthouse."

I thought for a moment about why she might go to the courthouse. We now had Rural Free Delivery, and the mailman came by about once a week. A few days earlier, Mother had received an official-looking letter, which she took to her bedroom to read privately. I wondered if the letter had prompted this trip.

Not finding any satisfying answers, I let the question go and started thinking about my new little wicker basket. I hoped to pay a visit to the general store and look through the sewing notions, but Mother did not say a word about going to a store. I did not dare bring it up.

When we arrived at Babi's, Mother went in the house while I took the horses around back. I pumped water into a tub for them to drink and drew some oats out of the wooden box by her little barn. Once they were watered, fed, and secured to a post, I went in the back entry. Mother was just leaving through the front door. She planned to walk the few blocks to the courthouse.

I was glad to see Babi. She poured tea into pretty china cups and brought out a plate of her sugar cookies for us. She showed me her sewing machine and then gave me a silver thimble. It just fit my finger! Finally, something new for my sewing basket! For a few moments, I forgot the lump in my stomach and the cloud over my head.

Mother came back to the house just before noon, flushed and excited.

"Well?" Babi asked her.

"The deed is done. The papers are signed," Mother stated as she took her hat off and laid it on a stand by the front door. "The judge saw reason. He gave me the farm…and most everything else."

Babi sat back in her rocking chair, her thick hands folded complacently.

"All of this is a shameful thing Vincent brought on our family," she commented. "You should get everything. You have five children."

Six children, I thought. Babi had already shaken Joe off the family tree.

After cutting a swath with Father, Babi turned on Mother and mowed her down like a field of hay. "For your part, you must go see the priest and make things right with the church." Babi's voice was quiet, steely. Mother started to protest, but Babi raised her hand. "Perhaps you could wear widow's clothes to show your remorse."

A look passed over Mother's face that betrayed hurt and anger at once.

"I don't need to grovel before the priest," Mother said a little too loudly. "The church hasn't shown a bit of compassion. Moreover, I will not wear mourning clothes when my husband is not dead. He chose alcohol over me and his children," Mother countered.

"The church's role is to point the way to God. Even in hard times, we must have the true compass the church provides," Babi lectured. "Just as you discipline your children, we as adults must be shown the error of our ways."

"And what was my error?" Mother snapped. "I tried to have a happy life and failed? That I was married by a judge rather than in the church? I was not the first American to shed the rules of the state church of Bohemia. Many of us want to figure out where the church ends and God begins. Besides, since I married outside the church, it seems that now the church would welcome me back." Mother paced as she made her points.

I shrank down on a footstool near the window, trying to make sense of their conversation. They had completely forgotten I was in the room.

"Oh, Mary, a divorce is a divorce, no matter whether you married in the church or not. You have broken God's law."

Divorce! Mother went to the courthouse to get a divorce? Was Father there? I wondered. *Why did she not tell me what was going on? I seethed. I was old enough to quit school and to do the work of a grown-up. She might have told me the family was being legally torn apart.*

Mother stormed over to the stair wall and pointed at an embroidered copy of the Ten Commandments written in Bohemian. Mother had learned to read and write in English, but she could still read a little in Bohemian.

"Let's see," she said as her finger wandered down the cloth. "No, I don't see the word 'divorce' in here. I do see 'Thou shalt not kill.' Perhaps I have prevented a murder by getting divorced. Think of that!"

Mother's finger tapped her chin. "If that's wrong and the church doesn't want me or my children, so be it." The silence that followed was as loud as a thunderclap.

Finally Babi spoke. "Mary, I can see how hard the past years have been." Her voice was low and soothing. Mother stood looking out the window, her chin quivering with rage. I was near enough to touch her, but I tried to make myself invisible. "You made a hard choice to end your marriage. I am only saying, take the next steps and make things right with God. And yes, with the church."

"I will make peace with God," Mother said as she turned to look at Babi. "And I'll make peace with the church as soon as it offers Christian charity."

Suddenly, the thimble dropped from my hand, *ding-dinging* across the hardwood floor. Both women looked at me. I ducked down to scoop up my treasure, wanting to avoid their stares.

"What are you going to tell the children?" Babi asked. She came over to me and pulled me up. We went to sit on the pretty green horsehair sofa.

"Bessie, here, never knows what is going to happen next." She held my chin, looked in my eyes, and frowned. "This child was so worried last year that she couldn't even eat. Seems to me that Eddie is a bit too old to be sucking his thumb. And does George still disappear with his friends every night? What about Carrie? Does she still bounce that ball for hours every day? And Bill, if ever a child was out of control, 'tis that little dickens. How are you going to help them get through this?"

"I'm giving them all guns to use if they see their father anywhere near the farm," Mother said recklessly. "They'll adjust easier if they think they can protect each other." She was looking right at me. A chill went down my spine. Mother's voice was strong, like a piece of fabric that cannot be torn.

"Your family is being destroyed," Babi said sternly.

"'Tis not!" said Mother, whirling around and reaching for her coat. "We'll be just fine."

Mother and I rode home in silence. I could not think of one question to ask her, and she probably would not have answered me. Then in midafternoon, Mother saddled up again and went to Moorland. I figured she went to see Mrs. Watson to drum up some business for the future when we had more cream and eggs again. I breathed a sigh of relief as she rode off.

As soon as Carrie, Eddie, and Bill came home from school, I called George into the house. "Let's go into the parlor. I have something to tell you," I said determinedly. Was it my place to tell my brothers and sister about the divorce? Probably not. However, as secretive as Mother had been, I figured someone had to clue them in.

"Today something happened that you all must know about. If Mother decides not to tell us, you will still need to know. Other people will find out."

Carrie rolled her eyes. "And everyone says *I'm* the dramatic one."

"I'm serious, Carrie. What happened today will affect the rest of our lives." Eddie sat on the couch and leaned against Carrie. For once, Bill was quiet. George stood looking out the window, his back to us.

I took a deep breath and told them about the trip to Fort Dodge and Mother's mysterious meeting. Then I repeated as best I could what Babi and Mother had talked about. I did leave out the part about shooting at Father if he came around. I finished by saying Mother thought we would get through this.

"She's right. We'll be okay," said George as he turned to face us. For the first time, I realized how grown-up he was at fifteen. He even had a little hair growing on his face, although I had never seen him shave.

"You weren't in the shop that day when Father went crazy with the gun," George said. "I was. Unless he quits drinking for good and forever, we cannot be around him. From what I hear, he is still drinking and still in a dangerous rage. We're better off without him."

We were all quiet for a while, thinking about what happened. Once you were divorced, I did not think you could be undivorced. Would we ever see Father again, even if he quit drinking? Did he think about us?

"Rumor has it that he might move back to Cedar Rapids," George said. "That's where he's from. Maybe he still has family there." Father had never talked about his family, and we certainly had never met anyone related to him.

"Divorced," Carrie moaned. "Our little family is *destroyed*. We'll never be the same." Eddie and Bill started to cry.

Suddenly Mother stood in the doorway. We had not heard her arrive. Her fur hat was still on her head, a brown envelope in her gloved hand, and a bulging saddlebag over her shoulder. "Our 'little family' won't be destroyed. We're going to do just fine," she said, looking at each of us in turn. "These are the divorce papers," she said, holding up the envelope. "We divided the property. Your father has no reason to come here anymore."

George stirred, and Mother looked directly at him. "The farm is mine and most of the property. He received some of the cattle and enough money to get along. We don't have to be afraid anymore," she emphasized again.

I frowned at the thought of Mother being afraid of anything. Now that I thought about it, she had been doing some things differently. For one, she stuck a table knife in her bedroom doorframe at night, so no one could open it from the outside. More than once, she had whirled around when I had quietly entered a room and surprised her. Because she had not said much, I had not thought about all the things we had done differently lately. Today was the first time she had left George alone on the farm or permitted me to go anywhere.

Now, she rummaged in the desk and found the key to lock the drawer where she kept important papers. As she stuffed the brown envelope in the drawer, she began talking again.

"We all have Spirek blood. We're strong, wise, and capable," she stated with more pride than assurance. "My ancestors lived under the worst tyranny, but they still managed to put away a nest egg. When they were able to leave Bohemia and the Austrian Empire, they moved here and bought land right away. They helped each other, worked hard, and have done well. We will do fine also." She looked at George again. "We'll have to figure out how to handle spring planting. But for now, let's get the evening chores done."

George nodded and left to go outside. Mother took her saddlebag and went upstairs to change into a housedress. I wondered where I belonged. George needed help in the barn, but I worried about my younger siblings, who sat huddled on the couch. Then Carrie got up, lit the lamp, and picked up a book. She squeezed between Bill and Eddie in the circle of lamp light and began to read.

I put on my coat and dug in the wooden box in the corner for my cap, scarf, and gloves. When I let myself out into the chilly air, twilight had come. The western sky was as pink, orange, and lavender as the hollyhock dolls I had made only a few months earlier. It was perfectly quiet, except for the lowing of the cows. My footsteps crunched in the snow as I stood in the middle of the yard. After months of winter's howling winds and snowstorms, there comes a moment when its defenses are down, and a sense of spring creeps in.

I turned all the way around. I could see to the horizon in every direction, and the worries of the day seemed small compared to the vast and beautiful prairie.

The dingy gray snow covering the prairie was the opposite of a summer day I remembered when we had a family picnic along the Des Moines River. Someone had pushed me in the water with a huge splash. I went down, down into the water. It covered my head and became my whole world for a moment. Then my feet touched bottom, and I automatically pushed up. When I broke into the air again, the ripples moved away from me in a widening circle, but the rest of the river remained serene. The ripples only last for a few moments.

That, I thought, *is what life is like*. The cares of the day suddenly did not seem so big and overwhelming. In the stillness of the twilight, a peace came over me. For the first time in a long while, I began skipping. Had I ever skipped in the snow? I veered away from the barn and skipped once around the yard. It felt so good to move freely and to breathe in the icy air. It felt good to be alive!

The next day when the other kids were at school, Mother revealed the contents of the saddlebag. She brought it out at lunchtime, opened it up, and handed guns to George and me. Mine was a little Smith & Wesson .38. We held target practice behind the barn for the next several days.

13

February 1900

The longer February days brought more sunlight, and the snow began to melt. While we welcomed milder weather, it brought us new problems.

Hay for the livestock was running low, and we needed to bring in more from the yard where it was stored. When the ground was frozen, we hitched the team to the stoneboat for the trip to the hay yard. One of us climbed the haystack and pitched dried alfalfa down onto the stoneboat, which had runners like a sled. When the ground was dry, we used the same process, except we hitched the team to the hayrack, which had wheels. This time of year when the heavy Iowa soil began to thaw, it turned into a thick black goo. It was almost impossible to take either the stoneboat or hayrack anywhere.

One morning with the sun shining and a warm breeze blowing, Mother decided we needed to haul more hay before the ground became too soft. She and George moved the stoneboat to the hay yard in the morning. After lunch, Mother stood on a haystack pitching hay over the side, while George spread it around to make room for as much hay as possible.

Our family had always worked together, with Father and Mother doing the hardest work and the rest of us taking on the lighter chores. When we all did our part, things worked well, but we missed Father's help. It seemed to me the outside work was getting further behind all the time, even though we tried so hard.

Anyway, that afternoon, my job was to cook a pot of bean soup and make cookies to use up some sour cream. I stood at the kitchen table rolling out cookie dough when a shadow passed by the window. I looked up but could not see what had passed. It was odd that Mutt had not barked to announce that someone had arrived. Curious, I went to the window.

Father was there by the barn gate! He leaned down, opened the gate, and walked his horse into the barnyard. Then he rode over to the hay yard. Mutt followed him, tail wagging, but Mother and George had not seen him. When he got to the stack of alfalfa, Mother looked up, dropped the pitchfork, and put her hands on her hips. I could see by their gestures that they were arguing. Then Father got down from his horse and climbed the stack. He picked up the pitchfork and threw down some hay.

I let out a cry as I tried to decide what to do. Mother had coached George and me many times to get the gun if Father showed up. Feeling the urgency of the moment, I didn't bother to go upstairs and get my handgun. Instead, I ran to the sewing room and got out the shotgun.

I eased out the kitchen door, and stood quietly, the barrel of the gun pointing down. I could hear them arguing in Bohemian. George dropped his pitchfork and leaned forward as if he planned to jump up on the stack.

Mother tried to take the pitchfork away from Father, but he threw it to the ground. He gestured at the farm, pointing toward a part of a fence that had fallen down. Then he pointed toward the shop and the hay yard. He seemed to have a lot to say. Mother stood with her arms crossed across her coat. Even from the house, I could see the fear and rage on her face. Finally, she let loose, shouting at him and pointing to the road.

Father reached out and pushed Mother with both arms. She stumbled backward; her arms flung up and back as she fell over the side backwards. So much for new beginnings. Father had returned like a reoccurring nightmare. Then he jumped down from the stack and got the pitchfork. He quickly climbed the stack and started throwing hay down in large, quick movements. George started for

Mother, but Father began shouting at him. George looked toward the house then picked up his pitchfork and began shuffling hay around the flat surface again.

That is when I cocked the gun, raised it in the air, and pulled the trigger. The crack it made echoed off the buildings and was surely heard by the neighbors. Father and George looked toward the house. The kickback knocked me on my bottom where I sat stunned at what I had done. *God in heaven, help me*, I prayed.

Mother finally limped around the haystack. She looked toward the house as she dusted herself off with strong, sweeping motions that told me she was hotter than a boiling teakettle. Father looked away from me to Mother and started thrusting the pitchfork as if he wanted to throw it at her. She began walking backwards, shouting something at him. He stepped toward her and thrust the pitchfork at her again.

No doubt about it, Father was out of control! I got up and started to lift the gun to my shoulder again and then set it down. Instead, I ran across the yard, calling, "Mother! Mother! Come here!"

"Mother, go with Bessie," George said evenly, almost lightly. "Father and I can finish up."

"*Vypadni, ženská!*" Father said in Bohemian, with acid in his voice. "You get out, woman!"

I ran hard as I ever had run, across the yard and out to the hay yard. Mother was still backing away when I got to her. I looked up at Father, though I was almost blind with fear and did not really see him. I tried to mimic George's calm, but I was crying too hard. I grabbed Mother around her ample waist and turned her around. "Come on, come on," I urged.

Mother started walking away with me but kept looking back at Father. I knew she was ready to have an all-out battle with him, but she continued toward the house. I kept glancing over my shoulder at Father, ready to run for the gun if he started walking toward us. Then I had a new worry. I had not aimed the gun at Father, but Mother might if she saw the gun. She looked up at the house, and a new wave of fear swept over me.

However, instead of going for the gun, to my utter amazement, Mother exclaimed, "Bessie! You left the door wide open. What were you thinking, letting all the cold in?"

I pushed her through the door and slammed it shut behind us. My knees were so weak I could hardly stand. Mother and I were both trembling. I led her to a kitchen chair and put the coffeepot on the hot part of the cookstove. Then I helped her take her coat off and put a shawl around her.

Quickly I ducked outside and brought the shotgun in. Mother stared straight ahead and did not see what I was doing, so I rushed to the sewing room and hid the gun away.

Coming back into the kitchen, I said, "Whatever made Father come today?" My voice sounded a little thin and high, but just speaking aloud seemed to melt some of the tension in the air. "Did he just come and start working like he'd never left? Isn't that strange?" I asked myself as much as Mother. She did not answer.

The coffee finally heated up. After she downed a cup, she seemed steadier. "I don't know what's possessed him. I never thought he'd come here again," she said. Then her eyes got wild. "George is still outside with him!" She jumped from her chair and went to the window. George and Father were making their way back to the barn with the stoneboat.

Then she exclaimed, "Oh no! Here come the kids home from school. I don't know what he might do. He isn't one bit rational!" Mother was still rattled.

I opened the door and called to Carrie, Eddie, and Bill. "Come in quickly! I'm baking cookies." I had left a pan of unbaked cookies and a mess of cookie dough on the table. Now I grabbed the pan and put it in the oven, noticing I was still a bit shaky.

"How come Father is out here?" Eddie asked as soon as he was in the door.

"Take off your boots and hang your coats up," Mother said automatically. "I guess your father decided to come for a visit. I want you to be really good if he comes to the house," she added. I wondered if she had forgotten the gun.

Since I did not know what to do, I tried to act normal. When the cookies came out of the oven, we ate the first pan full. I put a second pan in the oven and stirred the beans. Mother and I kept stealing glances out the window.

Outside, George and Father took off their coats in the late afternoon sun. They unloaded the stoneboat and fed the cattle. The tension in the house seemed thick as ice and words seemed to freeze in our throats, but finally I spoke up.

"Maybe I should help with the milking," I said. "Carrie, you help Mother with the last pan of cookies and set the table." She nodded. I could almost see her thoughts. She wanted to know what was going on but did not dare ask. The boys went up to their room to do some schoolwork. I slipped up to the bedroom, pulled out my .38, and put in a bullet from my stock of two. The gun fit smoothly in my coat pocket.

"Well, Bessie, how's my girl?" Father asked when he saw me come out to the barn. He came over and gave me a hug. I looked frantically at George and prayed Father did not feel the bulge of the gun in my pocket.

Father let go and patted me on the back. "It feels good to be home," he said. "What's cooking for supper?"

I stared at him. Had he not just about killed Mother? Had he not seen me blast the air with a shotgun? An unlikely song shouted in my brain. "Row, row, row your boat, gently down the stream. Merrily, merrily, merrily, life is but a dream." Was this a dream? But no, I could smell sour alcohol on Father's breath. I needed to keep rowing.

"Umm, umm, bean soup," I finally stammered.

Just then, George stepped up. "Bessie, I think Father and I can finish up the milking. You feed the chickens and then go put supper on the table. Father and I will be in," George said in an easy way. I was amazed how he took charge, standing tall, but keeping his voice even.

I pumped a pail of water for the chickens and threw some feed in their pan. When I left, Father was diligently milking a cow. George slipped out with me.

"He must have been drinking before he got here," George said. "He's had a few swigs since then, but I think the bottle is about gone." He grinned, pulled a small bottle out of his coat, and poured its contents on the ground. I wondered how he had gotten it away from Father.

"Tell Mother he calmed down and probably won't hurt us. He'll want to sleep it off before too long." The idea of Father coming in the house sent a chill through me—and I gave George a questioning look.

"Yes," George said, reading my thoughts. "He's expecting to eat supper here. Anyway, tell Mother to sneak out and go to the neighbors before he comes in." His teeth began to chatter, the only sign of nerves that he showed.

I stared at George, wide-eyed. "You mean she should saddle up the horse or just walk over to the neighbors?" A biting breeze stung my fingers despite my wool mittens. It wasn't a good night to walk anywhere, and Mother was already favoring her hip after the fall.

"Tell her to walk to the neighbors right now, without him seeing her," George said, tossing his head in Father's direction. He tapped his chin as Mother did when she was thinking hard, perhaps to steady himself. "I will try to keep him out here a bit longer, but be quick. I do not think he will hurt us, but he blames Mother for taking away the farm. He may get roused up again if he sees her."

I turned around and trotted back to the house, slipping where new ice was forming now that the sun was setting. Mother stood by the window watching for me. As soon as I told her what George said, she put on her coat, hat, and boots.

"Take charge, Bessie. Feed your father his supper. And remember you know how to defend yourself," Mother advised me. *The gun*, I thought again with a shiver.

Mother limped out the door and disappeared into the gathering darkness. There was just a sliver of moonlight glinting off the late winter snow to help her find her way down the road. *Now the neighbors would have another tale about the Kloubec family*, I thought.

George was right. Father did come in. I turned the lamp light low as we took our places at the table. All of us kids sat stealing looks at him, but he ignored us as he ate some bean soup, bread, and cookies. No one said a word during the meal, and he never asked where Mother was.

I could not eat much and wondered if Father might scold me, but he didn't notice that either. After scraping the bottom of his bowl, he stumbled into the parlor. The hard work and alcohol were taking their toll. He sat in the chair we once thought of as his. Before long, a soft snore told us he was asleep.

I shooed the boys upstairs, while Carrie and I quietly cleaned up the kitchen. Father was still asleep when we finished, so I put a quilt over him and we tiptoed upstairs. I took a butter knife with me and wedged it in the bedroom door so Father could not break in.

"Why is he here?" Carrie whispered for the fiftieth time. "Tell me what happened!" We got ready for bed and snuggled under our quilts before I began. I told her how Father had ridden up as if he still lived here and how he had argued with Mother and threw her down. I told her George was the hero, calming Father down and staying with him. I whispered the story to Carrie until she grew drowsy and fell asleep. Then I crept out of bed and stashed the pistol under my pillow. I stayed awake all night.

When I could not bear it any more, I went downstairs and put wood in the cookstove and lit a fire. It was 5:00 a.m. I dipped water out of the pail and filled the coffeepot. I had never made coffee before, so I had to guess how many spoons of grounds to put in the pot, but it seemed to turn out all right. I went to the cellar, got a ring of sausage, and fried it up with some potatoes. About an hour later, Father came out.

"Mornin', Bessie," Father said.

I kept my back turned to the stove for the moment, wondering how much he remembered from the day before. Then I took a deep breath and turned to face Father. "Good morning. Do you want to try my coffee?"

He nodded. I filled a cup and then filled a plate for him. He lifted his fork, and his hand shook a bit.

The others wandered down and sat around the table. It was like a picture of a typical family breakfast, if you could not see fear and confusion on our faces. Father ate in silence and then got up. He stood bent over and slowly stood to his full height.

"I'll be off now," he said, smiling at us. "But I'll be back."

The comment was probably supposed to be reassuring. He acted as if it was a normal day and he was off to Callender on an errand, but the chill that settled over us was anything but normal. I struggled with confusion. The looks on the faces of my brothers and sister said they too wondered if we had all just dreamed up the tales about Father. Did he really send Joe away? Shoot up the shop? Try to stab Mother with a pitchfork just yesterday?

Then a sound confirmed that we were not dreaming and that our father was going mad. He had hitched up Mother's horse and little buggy and was leaving with it. The little rig was Mother's pride and joy. Certainly, this would be another stick in the bonfire of Mother's anger and humiliation.

The kids did not go to school that day. Watching from the neighbor's window, Mother saw Father drive away. They gave her a ride home. What did they think of our family? The strange son who was sent away, the divorce, and now Mother pitifully showing up on their doorstep on a winter night. I had to keep wondering because Mother did not say a word about her little overnight trip, though she surely looked tired out.

Later that morning, George hitched the team up and took Mother to Fort Dodge to see the sheriff. We had instructions to put a chair against the door if Father returned. Heavens, we did not even have a lock on the door. That day, Mother got a restraining order saying Father could not come near the farm or any of us anymore, and George installed locks.

14

March 1900

Mother's hip bothered her for a long time after the haystack debacle. Her gloomy mood cheered up a bit the day her horse and buggy were returned to her none the worse for wear. Still, it took weeks before we could settle back to any kind of order. We were all jittery.

One morning I came downstairs to find Mother throwing something in the cookstove.

"What are you doing?" I asked, spying my photo album on the table.

"I'm burning the photos," Mother retorted.

I kept the album in the sewing room. Because visiting a photography studio was expensive, we just owned a few photos that I had carefully placed on the pages. Mother had apparently decided to get rid of the past by destroying photos of her wedding day and those of our family taken a few years earlier.

"No, don't do that!" I ran to the stove and grabbed at the edge of a photo. Mother tried to push me away, but I held on to the burning photo and backed away, blowing on it. I ran upstairs, intending to hide it away, but the scorched pieces were not worth saving.

I was thankful she hadn't destroyed my beautiful new album, but I mourned the loss of those photos. At that time, I could still picture Father and Joe clearly in my mind; but eventually, they faded away until I only saw them in the faces of my other brothers, all of whom bore a family resemblance.

With the restraining order now in effect, we might have relaxed a little, but the tense moments continued. I must have looked out the window a hundred times a day, wondering if I would see Father riding up the road or through the yard. I felt as nervous as a chicken who knows a fox is in the neighborhood. I understood how close we were to disaster. One more incident like the last one might mean the end of our family.

The effects of all this showed up slowly in the younger kids. It was not until later that we realized we had completely forgotten Eddie's birthday. He was born on Father's birthday, so we usually celebrated both at the same time. Poor Eddie. I knew how he felt, but at least I had been older when everyone forgot my birthday. Eddie turned eight that February.

Mother tried to make it up to him a month later by buying him a book and we made a special poppy seed cake for him, but those belated efforts did not seem to cheer him up. From that winter on, Eddie withdrew to another world, as though in his heart he had moved far away, where the turmoil could not touch him.

I tried to be the big sister for everyone, but for land's sake, I had no peace or wisdom to give anyone else. One moment I wished Father back, and the next moment I would break out in a sweat, reliving the whole sordid haystack episode.

I lost my appetite again and had trouble sleeping. I wanted to lie on the floor, scream, and kick my feet like a baby having a tantrum. I tried to hold it all in, but sometimes my anger and frustration popped out of me. I could really crack those rugs when I shook them out. But most of the time, I kept a tight rein on my feelings by focusing on other things, like my sewing. Many nights I sat up late, hunched over a piece of fabric, squinting in the dim lamp light. I finished every one of those aprons I was making.

In late March, I had a day of reckoning with myself. The robins were back, and the sun pierced the winter chill, making the air soft. I looked outside and saw the hope of spring. Then I went flying out the door, letting it bang shut behind me. I ran, lifting my long skirt enough so I could move freely. Mutt loped along beside me. His ears flapped charmingly, and he panted, unaccustomed to the exercise. I ran north up the road, away from the school and toward Moorland. I ran until my side ached and I was all out of breath.

The farm was long out of sight when I stopped, bent over at the waist, and tried to catch my breath. It was so quiet. I stood up and heard nothing but the rippling of grass in the faint breeze and the occasional call of a meadowlark. My racing thoughts slowed. The haystack episode had settled forever the fact that Father had to leave. None of us could bear the terror he brought. The truth was he was close to killing someone. Those simple thoughts came clearly as I stood on the road in the warm spring sunlight. It felt good to recognize the truth.

Finding a big rock, I sat down. A meadowlark sang nearby. Mutt stopped to lap water from the ditch and then flopped down at my feet for a nap in the sun. Some industrious ants working on a building project reminded me that I sometimes felt like an ant carrying a great big load on my back. I was not yet a teenager, but I felt as old as my mother.

I'd blamed myself for what had happened to our family, as though I could change things by being good or eating my food or not having bad thoughts about taking care of Joe. But on that clear spring day, I could see the problems in my family were not my fault. Father did not drink because I picked at my food. It was not my fault that he got hurt or that they sent Joe away. It was not! It was not my fault! I could not have changed what happened.

Just when I began to breathe easier, another thought came to me. I *was* guilty. I resented Father for pulling me out of school and for being cruel. I was angry with Mother for not telling me about the divorce before it happened. I hated her for playing dirges and ignoring Father as he tormented us kids. I despised the neighbors who gossiped about us. I was jealous of my cousins for having a better life than I did. I even despised the church for turning a cold shoulder to my family when we needed help the most.

Oh, I could hardly think of all the blaming I had done this past year. Then I remembered all those days when my attitude was "poor me." I felt so sorry for myself I could not see what the rest of the family was going through. I certainly had not made it better for anyone. I had not tried to bring any joy to Christmas and, land's sake, I forgot Eddie's birthday.

I was hardly the one to be pointing fingers at others because my own thoughts and actions shamed me. I buried my head on my lap and in a thin voice said, "God, I've sinned in thought, word, and deed. Forgive me." I had never said anything more heartfelt in my life.

No circumstance changed that spring morning. Yet I felt easier as I walked toward home, Mutt at my side. Once at home, I was hungry enough to eat a good lunch.

15

April 1900

In 1900, my birthday landed on the day between Good Friday and Easter Sunday. I was turning twelve. I might have pretended it was not a big deal, but there was no way Carrie was going to let Mother forget this year.

Money was tight, but Mother came up with some fabric from the cupboard and secretly made me a new white ruffled shirtwaist and blue skirt. She also bought me a red heart-shaped brooch. Carrie wrapped the packages in white tissue paper and laid them on the table by my plate at breakfast time. Mother, Carrie, George, Eddie, and Bill sat around the table and watched me carefully unwrap the gifts, which surprised and delighted me. I planned to wear all of them on Easter.

After the little party, we spent the day preparing to have Uncle Charles, Uncle Anton, their families, and Babi for Easter dinner. She had written to Mother asking her to take her turn in hosting Easter dinner. Mother did not like the idea. Moody and depressed, she had taken Babi's advice and begun wearing black dresses. She spoke as though she were a widow. If you did not know better, you would have thought Father had died. She did not go anywhere now, except to town to deliver cream and eggs.

I think her family worried about her and decided to come to us because Mother likely would not go to their homes to celebrate. We wouldn't be going to the Easter service because the church had excommunicated Mother. I guessed we were sinners and not good enough to sit with the "good" people. That thought brought me even more shame. It felt as if the church had opened the door and thrown us out on our bottoms.

The Spirek relatives seemed to be mulling over what they thought of the divorce. I was sure they did not all agree on the matter, but at least Anton and Charles had decided to let kindness rule because they were coming to our house for the highest holy day, Easter.

Of course, we cleaned every room from the ceiling to the farthest corner of the floor. We scrubbed the winter's coal soot off every wall, washed and waxed the floors, and dusted and polished the parlor furniture. The spring cleaning took a week, and we finished on Easter Saturday. Water boiled on the stove all day for one project or another. Mother baked rolls and a pretty cake with vanilla frosting. We boiled eggs for potato salad and for dyeing in bright Bohemian colors. Only after that did the serious cooking begin.

On Easter morning, Mother sent George and me out to do the chores while she put our last big ham in the oven and mixed up the potato salad. We had a quick breakfast of Easter bread and boiled eggs. Then we set the tables for dinner and rushed around, making sure everything was perfect until our company arrived. I felt special in my new outfit and looked forward to being with family again. I had hardly seen my cousins in the last year. We were slipping away from each other, like two buggies going in opposite directions.

How excited we were to see them coming up the road! Altogether, there were six adults and about twenty cousins. After everyone arrived, I brought out the aprons I had made for my girl cousins and aunts. I had even wrapped them in white tissue paper tied with pink ribbons. I can still hear their exclamations as they opened their gifts. I had made full-sized aprons for the teenagers and grown-ups and tiny aprons for the little girls. I put rickrack on some of the edges and embroidered others. The pockets were in contrasting colors. Everyone seemed happy with the gifts.

Uncle Anton led us in a special prayer. The adults sat at the big table in the kitchen, while the rest of us used a makeshift table set up in the parlor. Some of the little kids were too excited to eat, so they just ran around, while others sat on their mothers' laps. Carrie and I washed and dried dishes and kept the platters and bowls filled with food during the first shift. When the adults finished eating, Mother and my aunts took over the duties, and Carrie and I sat down with our plates heaping.

It was a happy day, that Easter. The sun hinted at the warmth of summer, so we kids were outside most of the time. With all the chatter, good food, and cousins running around, I forgot for a few moments that Father and Joe were not there.

New life was everywhere. My little cousins toddled around, delighted to be together. In the pasture, new calves leapt and played. Baby kittens purred next to their mother in the warm sunshine outside the barn. Little green sprouts popped out from their brown winter blankets. Yellow and purple wildflowers bloomed across the yard. We smiled and cooed at a litter of baby pigs, a flock of fluffy yellow chicks, and our odd-looking young guinea hens. I thought that maybe spring was God's way of showing us the Easter resurrection in a way we could understand.

Later in the afternoon, Emma and I walked up the road. I turned to smile at her, but her words brought me back to reality. She meant well, surely. All she did was ask where Father was. Still, it brought that lump back into my stomach.

"I don't know for sure," I said. "We think he went back to his hometown, Iowa City." Mother had heard that rumor one day when she delivered cream to her friend's house in town.

"Do you miss him?"

Did I? How can a young girl not miss her father? I wanted him to wink at me again and tuck me under his arm as he relaxed in his chair. I wanted him to take care of our family again, but every thought of him got tangled up in horrible pictures of him grabbing Joe around the neck or being hauled off in a wagon after he shot up the shop or, more recently, shoving Mother. Those pictures closed me up like having a goose-feather pillow over my face.

I couldn't share any of that with Emma, not even a flat-toned factual account, so I just shrugged. Emma seemed to take that as a sign that I did not care.

"Father says we should pray for his soul," she elaborated.

She was wandering into territory so painful to me that I felt like she was using a scrub brush on an open wound. I did not know how to pray for my own soul, let alone Father's. My face burned, and tears pushed at my eyes.

"Oh, look," I said, turning away to point at a field. A mother duck was swimming in a pothole with four ducklings behind her. We stood and watched for a while and then turned around and walked silently back to the farmstead.

It was then that I knew things could never be the same again. The distance between my cousins and me was too great. I could never utter to them the painful memories locked in my heart nor trust anyone with that tender part of myself.

Not that I was alone in my pain. Mother, George, Carrie, Eddie, and Bill carried the same horrors and shame. The same secrets. We did not talk about the past with each other because we did not need to. The shared pain bound us together and pulled us away from everyone else as each of us in our own way tried to heal the wounds to our hearts.

A few weeks later, events began to help us move on from that dark winter. One day when Mother delivered cream and eggs, her friend told her how the Chicago Great Northern planned to lay track right through Moorland. The workers lived in railroad cars, but the managers needed housing. Mother's friend was building a new boarding house. Before she left that day, Mother agreed to run the boarding house. The deal happened so fast that it took us all by surprise.

Mother told us the news late in the afternoon when she came home from town. I was washing fresh garden lettuce in the house, and Carrie was fussing about having to pick the pinfeathers from the prairie chickens George had brought home for supper.

We were stunned to silence. I just stared at Mother. Carrie's mouth worked like it needed some warming up in order to spit out any words. Finally, at the supper table, we began to ask questions. What would happen to the farm? Would we live at the boarding house? I already knew why Mother had taken this impulsive step: we could not handle the farm come summer, and we were running low on cash.

The idea of moving was a shocking turn of events, so when Carrie complained about not feeling well, we just figured the news was too much for her. She slipped out of her chair, her food untouched, and went upstairs to bed.

Mother went upstairs later and found Carrie burning with fever and covered with a red rash. She whispered hoarsely that her throat was sore. Mother sent me up with cold water and a washcloth to try to bring the fever down. We took turns all night caring for her. The next day was no better, nor the next. She lay listlessly in bed, the glands in her neck swollen thick as a wool scarf and her breath coming in short, shallow bursts.

All the decisions Mother needed to make about the farm waited, even though she planned to open the boarding house in just a few weeks. Now she focused on saving Carrie. Finally, Mother sent George into Fort Dodge to get the doctor and to inform Babi about Carrie and about the move.

The doctor arrived the next morning. He examined Carrie and shook his head. "Her symptoms point to two diseases. Scarlet fever or diphtheria. Can't be sure which it is. They both cause fever, rash, and sore throats."

He stroked his beard thoughtfully. "My guess is it is diphtheria." With that, he pulled some medicine out of his bag and gave it to Mother. His parting words were that he did not know if Carrie would survive.

When I heard that, it was as if a baseball had hit me. Life without Carrie? What would that be like? We had already lost Joe and Father. We had almost lost Mother. The thought of losing Carrie made me feel as though someone had set me ablaze with kerosene and I myself might die of the inescapable pain. I went to our bedroom and knelt down. Carrie lay still, her eyes closed.

"Carrie! Carrie! If you can hear me, you have to get better. Hear me? Please get better!" I begged. The rest of the family crowded into the bedroom. I knew we were all silently praying for a miracle. I took

Carrie's hand in mine and vowed not to let go until she was better. I stayed there for hours.

Sometime during the night, I felt Carrie stir. I had fallen asleep kneeling with my head on the bed. Mother had draped a shawl over my shoulders. By the dim lamp light, I could see Mother now slept sitting up in a straight-backed chair, her mouth gaping open. I still held Carrie's limp hand.

"Bessie," she whispered. "Do you believe in angels?"

"Carrie! For land's sake, you are talking! Are you better?" She felt cooler. Perhaps her fever had broken.

"I'm so sleepy," she said and drifted off to sleep. I crawled into bed with her, tucking my icy feet gratefully into the soft bedding. A while later, she spoke again. "Bessie, I saw an angel. He kind of waved over me and said that he was giving me the right medicine. Then he said, 'Be plucky.'"

"So an angel told you to be plucky." I had to snicker. "Angels don't talk to people."

"This one did," she mumbled as she slipped off to sleep again. Whether I believed her angel story or not, her fever broke, and she began to improve.

Lying in bed whispering with Carrie had been a routine for as long as I could remember. This night, I hugged myself with joy as I realized we would have more time together as sisters. And I thanked God who heard my desperate prayers.

Carrie recovered, but weeks passed before she was plucky enough to get out of bed. Meanwhile, we made plans to move. A neighbor rented our land. Soon he brought his team over and began planting a crop. George planned to stay on at the farm to tend the animals. We took one cow, Ada, to town, for Mother had shrewdly sold it to the owner of the boarding house. It became my job to milk the cow. In time, we planned to sell the other animals.

Mother figured to sell the farm too. Our precious farm, which held all the hopes and dreams for our family just a few years ago, was going to be gone. For now, Mother and I just packed our clothing and personal items in a couple of trunks.

The year before when Father gave me the three-cornered veil, it was a sign that we were a family again, a normal family that lived together and went to church together. I did not know what I believed about church anymore, as I felt as if it had disposed of us without much concern. But even though the veil was related to church attendance, it was filled with meaning and I decided to keep it. I carefully folded it in a piece of gingham cloth. If Mother found it, surely she would toss it in the stove and destroy this reminder of Father and the church.

I placed the veil at the bottom of my little wicker sewing basket and laid the thimble from Babi on it, along with some thread and a little pincushion. Tears filled my eyes. In a way, the tiny basket was my treasure chest. I put the lid on the basket and tucked it deep in the trunk next to my sabotaged photo album and the handgun.

The public rooms of the new boarding house were furnished, but we moved in our own beds and dressers with the help of my uncles. It was quite a house, the grandest one in Moorland. I loved the gleaming white paint and the sunny south-facing windows. The inside smelled like fresh-sawed wood. Inside, the stairway to the second floor was so grand it took my breath away.

Mother had sent Carrie to stay with her sister, Aunt Anna Koll, while she recovered from her sickness. Now, I wished Carrie could see the staircase, knowing it would impress her, but she stayed with Anna all summer.

Even the yard at the boarding house with its sapling trees, smoke house, and tiny barn seemed nice. We staked Ada on the edge of town each day, so she could eat plenty of fresh grass. I milked her in the morning and walked her to the edge of town. In the evening, I went to get her and milked her again.

Our boarding house became a headquarters for railroad managers. However, if the boarding house was grand, my role was not. I worked right alongside Mother, cooking and cleaning, although we hired someone to do the laundry, including all the bedding. Our family had two bedrooms on the main floor, next to the kitchen. I stayed in Mother's room, and the boys had the other one.

I liked living in town, having neighbors close by and visiting with other girls. There were many things to do in a town like Moorland, which had a population of about two hundred people in 1900.

I soon convinced Mother that even if she wore black and seemed to be in mourning, I needed to go places and do things. The friends I made in Moorland were more accepting than the country kids were. I did not feel the same stigma I had on the farm.

Sometimes in the afternoon, after I had done my chores and before we started cooking the evening meal, I went for a walk near the edge of town. Even though I was supposed to get Ada, I poked along, not anxious to return to the boarding house. I even had a special rock where I sat. From my perch, I could look across the flat prairie, almost to our farm, it seemed.

I'd sit very still, aware of the little things around me: the slight breeze blowing the grass, a bee buzzing by, the scent of sweet clover in the early summer air, robins chirping across the way. I could see the big blue sky studded with fluffy clouds or a rain cloud coming up in the west, but I wished I could see the horizon better. It always appeared blurry.

My life was like that too. How I longed to drop into my life in ten years, when I was twenty-two, just for a few moments so see how my life turned out. Would I still live in Webster County? Would I still be working for Mother at the boarding house or would I be married and have children of my own? Would Father be around? Surely, if I could jump into the future for a few minutes, I could tell how things turned out, and I'd have a better idea of how to handle life between here and there.

One day while I sat on my rock, a butterfly landed on the palm of my hand. I could feel the light tickle of its tiny feet. Poor butterfly, wandering into a situation it did not foresee—into the powerful grip of something that could crush it. Was the butterfly deciding whether to stay on my hand or leave? I left my palm open and watched.

After a few seconds, the flutter of yellow lifted off my hand and dipped and zigzagged across the prairie. Maybe, I thought, I was like that butterfly. I could stay sad and upset with Joe being gone, fearful of my father, angry over the divorce. On the other hand, I could let go and move on.

The butterfly was so free. Maybe I too needed to let go of the past and move on. Rather than making myself sick over the divorce, I could hope Joe was happy and Father would get well. Maybe this was the beginning instead of the end. Maybe if God took care of butterflies, He could also take care of Joe, Father, and even me. Had I not come down this same road of thought months ago? Yes, sitting by the creek bank with Eddie, I had chosen to look for the good side of things.

I looked out again across the prairie. Even if the future was not any clearer than the horizon, I could practice hoping for the best every day. The past year had gone faster than it seemed possible. No doubt, the future would be here as quickly as I could skip on home. My heart smiled at the thought.

PART II

The Kloubec children, circa 1903
Bessie, Edwin, George, Carrie & Bill

16

December 1903

Life changed a lot when we moved to the boarding house in Moorland in 1900. Mother planned to keep four rooms for boarders and cook up breakfast and supper seven days a week. But from the start, things galloped ahead of us like a bunch of runaway horses. We had landed in town in the midst of the big railroad boom. All we could do was hang on and try to steer in the right direction. We never managed to get control of things.

Mother started with a tidy plan, beginning with the menu. On Sunday mornings, we'd bake our good caramel rolls made with cream, butter, and brown sugar. The rest of the week, we planned to serve sausage and flapjacks, which were hearty, cheap, and easy to cook.

She planned to put a big ham in the oven for Sunday dinner. The ham bone became the base for Monday's bean soup. Tuesday we would fry chicken, and on Wednesday and Thursday, the scent of roast beef or pork filled the house all afternoon. Fridays we would serve wild game or fish. The week would wrap up on Saturday with fried steak.

Real life was quite a bit messier. Sometimes we had extra eggs, so we scrambled them for breakfast. Sometimes there were no eggs at all, so we were the ones scrambling.

Usually, you could set your clock by when the farm lady brought chickens in for us at noon on Tuesdays, but if there was a storm and she could not get to town, the menu changed. Or if the fish were not biting on Fridays, we had to scare up something else fast. Ducks, prairie chickens, and catfish were the most common meals on Fridays. The fish and game were supplied by my brothers, who went hunting or fishing, and sometimes a local fellow stopped by to sell us his catch of the day. When we were hunkered down in the winter, we served salted cod shipped to Iowa in wooden boxes. Oh, the menu plan could go amuck fast. So did all the other plans.

As I mentioned, most of our boarders were railroad officials. The guest rooms were on the second floor. We planned to put two to a bed, as was common, but with the northwest Iowa railroads competing with each other in laying track, we often had up to sixteen boarders instead of eight. Mother was smart and bought an extra bed for each room. In the blink of an eye, our profits doubled. The men were glad to sleep four to a room for the same price because there was nowhere else to go.

Of course, twice as many boarders meant twice as much work: twice as many potatoes to peel, dishes to wash, chamber pots to empty. The boarders paid extra to have a lunch made up to take with them each day. We learned to move fast to get all the work done.

Mother planned that the boarders would eat in the dining room, while the family occupied the kitchen table. She had not reckoned that other people in town also needed a place to eat, so we provided breakfast and supper for quite a crowd. When you have to eat in shifts, keep setting tables, and washing dishes, you do not pay much attention to who sits where. Besides, I rarely got to sit down to a meal.

In the end, I figured we made breakfast and dinner over a thousand times each, for an average of thirty people each time, not including filling lunch buckets. And I had milked Ada and later her replacement, Lady, two thousand times. Carrie, Eddie, and Bill helped out before and after school; but George worked for a farmer, and we did not see much of him.

I tried to find a few moments for myself each day. I loved to look for tiny violas, crocuses, or other pretty flowers on the prairie or in the backyard among the thriving young oaks. Then I would forget about Mother and the boarding house and Father and Joe for a few moments.

Most of those years at the boarding house, Mother wore a black skirt and shirtwaist. The townspeople seemed to accept that she was deeply grieved that her marriage had ended. In fact, I am sure after a couple of years they doubted their own minds. Was she a scandalous divorcee or the Widow Kloubec? She certainly acted the widow. Maybe that is why the townspeople treated us so kindly.

Carrie would probably humph at that. She would say people in those days blamed widows and orphans for their situation. That was sometimes true, but I still think there were many kindnesses shown to us those years in Moorland. For instance, for the most part, the boarders behaved themselves. If a fellow seemed to be drinking a bit much or getting out of line in any way, he would suddenly be moving out. I am not sure who took care of those things, the townspeople, railroad officials, or Mother, but we did not worry much about unsavory characters.

Many of the boarders missed their own families, and they enjoyed being around us kids. They often helped Bill with his sums or taught Eddie a new song on the piano. As for Carrie and me, Mother strictly instructed us on proper behavior with so many men living there. It helped that our family quarters were tucked away off the kitchen. We need not have worried though. The worst the boarders ever did was to say a cuss word, miss the spittoon, or stay too long at the saloon. In a typical evening, a group of them would gather at the dining room table to play cards or in the parlor to smoke cigars until bedtime.

These men came from all kinds of different places. Just listening to them talk about faraway places, people, and politics was an education. President Theodore Roosevelt was a big topic of conversation. No one had ever seen the likes of him. He was the hero of the Spanish-American War as well as a rich man who wanted to give everyone a "square deal." They filled my head with tales about "Teddy" and his Rough Riders in the Badlands so that my first impression of Dakota was that it was a wild frontier filled with cattle, cowboys, and criminals.

Settled now in our little Iowa village, the years rolled by. Suddenly I was fifteen and wondering if I would spend the rest of my life cooking and cleaning in the boarding house. It seemed like a lifetime since we had moved to Moorland, and the future looked to be laid out as clearly as the little brick path to the outhouse.

Then one day, Mother went into her bedroom and sewed herself a lavender blouse. Land's sake, I was so used to her drab mourning clothes that I could hardly believe my eyes. After that, she sewed a white shirtwaist and began wearing a sparkly brooch Babi had given her. Was it my imagination, or did she have more color in her cheeks?

It was not until I came upon her lingering over a cup of coffee in the kitchen with one of the boarders that I began to understand. Understand? Well, let us say it threw me into a tizzy. In my wildest imagination, I could not believe an old woman of thirty-eight with a brood of kids and a boarding house to run would be inclined toward romance. However, as I paid closer attention, it became apparent that Mother was sweet on Mr. Roots, and it looked like he was sweet on her.

My mother having a romance made me chuckle as I dusted the parlor or milked the cow. I felt my spirits lift with the idea, but I kept my observations to myself. I did not know much about Mr. Roots, except he came from Missouri and was in the restaurant business in Rockwell. Most of his customers were railroad crews that worked west of us. How he came to stay at our boardinghouse, I do not know.

He always talked and joked with my brothers, making their lives a little happier. He was helpful too. He did not mind fixing a broken window for Mother or repairing a chair or shoveling snow away from the door.

That is just how easy we began to think of Albert Roots as part of the family. Those months were, as they say, all sunshine and roses. One time he insisted on taking the whole family to Fort Dodge, where we had our photos made. We each had our own picture taken, and the five of us kids posed together. Then, oddly, he and Mother posed together.

He came at the right time for other reasons too. Providing services during the railroad boom time was profitable, and Mother's bank account was bulging. She also owned the farm where we had lived, though it still had a mortgage. A businesswoman at heart, she wanted to invest her extra money.

In the evenings, Al Roots and the other boarders traded tales of what was happening across the country. When he and Mother sat having a late cup of coffee, they would talk in low, excited voices about what the future might hold. Al Roots suggested investing in land in North Dakota, which had only been a state for fifteen years and where some of the boarders had contacts, including one who owned some land there.

Mother began going for drives with Mr. Roots on Sunday afternoons. I did not know where they went, but as long as she was out of the house, I had a few hours of freedom. Often I spent that time at the dining room table, a jar of ink at my elbow, a fountain pen in hand, and some of Mother's good linen paper in front of me. I wrote letters to Babi, Aunt Annie, and my girl cousins.

I missed seeing Babi, who had suffered a stroke and hardly left her house in Fort Dodge anymore. Aunt Anna and Uncle Joseph Koll moved in with her. I only visited Babi once in those years, although I tried to write her the news at least once a month. Mother was not much at writing letters.

April 1902

Dear Babi,

I hope you are doing well. We are enjoying the spring weather. Everyone is fine, except Bill skinned up his knee. We took all the mattresses and pillows out this week and gave them some air and sun. Next week we will take the rugs out and beat them. That is a dirty job. I have not had much time to sew. Mother said Carrie and I can take the train to Fort Dodge to see you this summer.

Love,
Your granddaughter, Bessie Kloubec

Aunt Annie remained my favorite, though I hardly ever saw her either.

January 1903

Dear Aunt Annie,

Thank you so much for the silk stockings! My first pair. It did not seem like Christmas without seeing family, so your package was doubly welcome. As usual, we cooked for many people who could not go home for Christmas. We had the oven full of roasting geese and cooked a whole ham on top of the range. There were not any leftovers. How I wish you would come to visit us in your Austrian bobsled as you did when we lived on the farm.

Fondly,
Your niece, Bessie Kloubec

I did not know why we saw so little of the Spireks after the divorce. To this day, I wonder if it was not just easier to avoid each other. It warmed my heart to remember all the Fourth of July and Christmas celebrations we used to have, although I sometimes felt sad that the friendships with my girl cousins seemed like a distant dream. Little did I know that distance was about to grow.

One October morning in 1903 when I came in with a pail of fresh milk, Mother was humming a tune around the kitchen. She smelled sweet like she had used her special lilac talc, and her hair was all done up in her best holiday style. Land's sake, she even wore her lavender shirtwaist and good black suit. It wasn't until she put on her hat, the dark maroon one with the outrageous plume on top, that she informed me that our lives were about to change forever.

"Bessie, you'll have to take over for the rest of the day. Have Carrie set the tables when she gets home and be sure the boys help with kitchen cleanup tonight. Mrs. Sumpter will stop in to check on you after the supper hour."

I dared not ask where she was going, although my mind reeled with questions.

"I'll be back tomorrow," she said, a funny little smile twitching at her lips.

"Tomorrow!" The word jumped out of my mouth with surprising force and no direction from me.

There was a long pause before she crooned, "Al and I are going to be married."

My mouth dropped open, and I could not make any words at all come out for a few moments. Finally, I managed to croak, "You're marrying Mr. Roots?"

"That's right," she said, a smug smile spreading on her face. "We're taking an overnight honeymoon trip and will be back tomorrow." She looked as pleased as a kitty cat who just found a dish of cream.

Just then Al Roots walked in the front door. There was an awkward silence, as he must have guessed Mother was just getting around to telling me about the marriage plans. She turned and smiled at him. He picked up her valise and offered Mother his arm, and they walked out the front door without remembering to say good-bye.

I myself whispered "Good-bye" after they were out of earshot and then danced around the room, trying to take in this surprising turn of events. I wanted so badly to tell someone that I put aside the long list of jobs and flew out the door as soon as they jingled around the corner with the horse and buggy. Going over to the livery stable where we kept our riding horse, I saddled up and lit out for our old farm to see George. I still went to my big brother for reassurance whenever my world did a flip. We hashed out the amazing turn of events as we sat on the farmhouse porch catching the golden warmth of the fall sun.

When the newlyweds got back the next day, Al Roots moved right into Mother's bedroom, and Carrie and I began sharing a cot in the hallway. A few weeks later, he quit the restaurant business. He said business was slow in the winter, and he wanted to travel around and look for some good land. In December, he took the train to

North Dakota. Every day he wrote Mother, outlining where he was and what kind of contacts he made.

His letters were enthusiastic, even though he was traveling in the coldest time of year. Somehow, he missed any snowstorms, although he said the snow was deep and he went by sleigh to see land. Within days of arriving back in Moorland, he had talked Mother into leaving her lucrative business and purchasing a farm in North Dakota.

Her giddy acceptance surprised me. Where was my tough-minded, no-nonsense mother? Who was this strange woman who tittered every time Al Roots said something funny? Who was this woman who overlooked undone chores and hugged her kids each day? Surely she was someone pretending to be Mother.

In addition, this strange woman seemed to submit to Mr. Roots's ideas about what to do with her finances. She jumped at the idea of leaving the moneymaking boarding house to go back to farming. Al Roots was suddenly the head of our family and making big decisions for us.

I found myself exchanging glances with Carrie and our brothers. Was this change in Mother for real? Would it last?

17

March 1904

In March 1904, we moved to Dakota. I was almost sixteen, and that train ride was the most exciting event in my whole life. We all dressed up in our traveling clothes, and when the conductor called, "All aboard!" we climbed the steps to the passenger car. Behind us, our possessions were loaded in emigrant boxcars, and our horses rode in a cattle car.

Carrie and I sat together in the lime green seats after we got done pressing our faces against the window glass, hungry for our last view of Moorland. The rumble of the train engine grew, and we began moving forward with a jerk. We craned our necks to see the familiar houses and shops as they slid past the window. In a few moments, we rattled out of town, and Moorland became smaller and smaller. When the track curved, the town disappeared completely.

I could not help staring at our images reflected in the window and note that I looked quite grown-up with my hair piled on my head. A fashionable ribbon dangled on one side from my rimless spectacles, so after years of seeing a fuzzy view of the world, I could pop my glasses on and actually see things. Mother said my eyes were the same color as cornflowers, but I was only five foot two, thin as a straw, and my hair was a boring dark brown. I thought my overall reflection in the glass was dismal, although Carrie called me "dainty" and wished aloud that she could shrink to my size.

At fourteen, Carrie was now taller than I was. She was so pretty with her flashing eyes, imposing brows, and thick dark hair. Where I was quietly mature, she enjoyed being the queen of drama.

"Good-bye, little town. I'll never see you again," Carrie said mournfully as the train gained speed. "Farewell to you, Babi. Good-bye, darling Joe. Oh, Father, I may never see you again." She settled back in the soft seat with a sigh.

"Land's sake, Carrie," I said, rolling my eyes. "Maybe you should sit in one of those seats that face backward so you can dwell some more on the past." I did not want to think about leaving our other Spirek relatives behind, let alone our grandmother, brother, and father. Best to look toward the future.

George, now almost twenty, rode in the emigrant car so he could take care of the horses and watch over our personal goods. I was surprised Mr. Roots did not take the post because it was common for the man in the family to ride there. I still called him mister even though after they had married, he said we could call him Al. None of us could bring ourselves to think of him as our father. Never would. Still, I had to admit life had improved since Mother met him.

Mr. Roots probably let George ride in back so he could enjoy some leisure time with Mother. I was just relieved George decided to move to North Dakota with us instead of staying in Iowa where he had made a life. As he got older, he reminded me a lot of Father when he was younger. He worked hard but loved to clown around and was quite popular.

Eddie, now twelve, was in the seat across from us using a leg clench to keep our youngest brother, ten-year-old Bill, in his seat. Eddie was frustrated already. No doubt, he would rather read a book or watch the scenery outside the window than wrestle with Bill.

Carrie was not finished talking about leaving Iowa and the rest of our family. "But they will be so far away!" Carrie whined.

I thought about Joe. He would be eighteen now. "Carrie, just remember we can write to Babi, just like we sent letters from Moorland to Fort Dodge. Joe is doing fine at Glenwood, and we can still send him packages from Dakota. And Father…" My voice trailed off.

Carrie looked down and gave the seat in front of us a hard kick.

"Carrie, stop kicking!" Mother ordered from the seat ahead of us. She sat with Mr. Roots.

A lot of rail ties covered the ground between Moorland, Iowa, and LaMoure, North Dakota. Even so, the distance we covered on that train trip in March 1904 was nothing compared to the distance our hearts had traveled in the last five years.

In 1899, I had been an Iowa farm girl with a sister, *four* brothers, a mother, and a father. We were part of the big Catholic Spirek family. Now I would be a North Dakota farm girl with a sister, *three* brothers, a mother, and a *step*father. We were no longer Catholic. In addition, we would not know a soul in the whole state, let alone have any relatives around. Thank goodness, no one had decided to change my name. I was still Bessie Emma Kloubec. If I felt a little bewildered inside, I did not let it show. Mother had not talked about our past in a coon's age and did not want us to either.

Packing for this move reminded me of packing to leave the farm. Once again, I had tucked my wicker sewing basket in a corner of the trunk, the beautiful picture album Mother gave me squeezed in next to it. Sometimes I opened the basket just to touch the little triangle of veil hidden there. I had wrapped my handgun in a soft cloth tucked underneath it all.

Every day on the train, Carrie went through her litany of woes. We would never see our brother Joe or Father again, and we would miss the Spirek family gatherings. At first, I tried to cheer her up; but finally, I decided she liked the drama of losing everything.

I liked the idea of beginning a new life. I wanted the pain of the past to go away like the tail end of a thunderstorm vanished over the eastern horizon. I really hoped we could leave our secrets behind.

Now, as we pulled the sandwiches and cookies out of a knapsack we packed for the trip, I remembered how tickled I was when my aunts and uncles came to Moorland the day before we moved. They brought Babi along to wish us farewell. She had hardly been out of bed since her stroke, so it meant even more that she traveled to see us before we moved so far away.

Still, even that day when our relatives chose to send us off on a high note, there were many unsaid words hanging in the air. They were meeting their new brother-in-law, Mr. Roots, for the first time, so there were a lot of handshakes, congratulations, and some sage advice from the menfolk.

Apparently, Mother had redeemed herself a bit with our relatives. She had her brothers' attention when they learned Mother had sold our eighty-acre farm to purchase three hundred and twenty acres in North Dakota. Owning land still increased your status in their Bohemian culture. Mr. Roots had brokered the deal, so I figured they held him in some regard. Mother even bragged a bit to her brothers that the farm in Cottonwood Township, North Dakota, cost $8,000. She paid for it with the farm in Iowa and a $2,840 mortgage.

It was probably good that the relatives did not know much about the Dakota bonanza farms that covered many sections of land. Why, rumor had it that a chicken farm just twenty miles north of our new place had forty thousand chickens. So much for the wild frontier I had first imagined.

I took a deep breath and came back to the present. We were swaying along in the train on our way to a new life. Out of Iowa, off to North Dakota. I needed to tuck the past away, like the gun hidden in the trunk.

That night as the train rocked along through the dark, I dreamed of my brother Joe. Five years had not erased my teeter-totter feelings of guilt and relief that he was locked away in an institution. I could not remember a time when people did not whisper about Joe. Feeling guilty, I thought if no one in North Dakota knew about Joe, maybe we would not have to face well-meaning people who implied some family sin caused Joe's fits.

Of course, Joe wasn't the only source of family scandal. Father's drinking and the violent episodes at our farm were well-known in the community. I think my parents' divorce just proved to some people that there was something dark about our family. On paper, my *parents* got divorced, but really, our *family* got divorced, because everything changed from that point on. I cannot begin to describe the shame of coming from a divorced family in a rural, Catholic community in 1900. I did not even know anyone else who was divorced.

Now, years later the disgrace and shame still caused bad dreams and made my stomach sick. To add to my mixed feelings, I still longed to fix our family and imagined springing Joe from the institution where he lived. What I would give to be tucked under Father's protective arm again. Sometimes when I saw a strange man around Moorland, I would look close to see if it was Father, lost and alone. Leaving Iowa without seeing them again was like quitting a book without reading the final chapter.

The dream about Joe opened up all those old feelings as the train rocked through the night. Slowly, I grabbed at each humiliating, horrifying thought. Like taking laundry off a clothesline and putting it away, I put my memories in a dark closet of my mind and shut the door.

Before I slept again, the eastern horizon showed a thin glowing line, like light showing under the door of a lit room. I reached out my hand toward it. Moving to a new life, I would do everything in my power to make sure our family disgrace was erased and the slate of shame wiped clean.

18

The train trip to Dakota took three days. Having never been on the other side of Fort Dodge, I could hardly take in the size of America. While Iowa was settled and the land cultivated, as we moved north, we saw fewer farms and towns. In Minnesota, snow spotted the brown prairie, but as we traveled farther north and west, it turned all white. The sky was vivid blue like Mother's good glass bowl. The white clouds rose to the top of the sky, like tall white mounds of whipped cream. However, in less than a moment, the sky could change to wash-water gray as a spring rain began.

We arrived at LaMoure on March 16. The cars carrying our belongings were switched to a siding and unhitched. The rest of the train chugged away as I stood in my winter coat and warm bonnet and watched it disappear out the west side of town. I had thought we were going to the ends of the earth; but now it occurred to me that the United States went far to the east, west, and south, and a whole other country, Canada, existed to the north.

My brothers and Mr. Roots unloaded the carriage and horses from the train cars. A drayman came by, and the men filled his wagon with some of our belongings. We climbed in the carriage and began a slow trot out of town, past a tall building with the date "1894" carved in the bricks. George rode one of the horses beside us.

LaMoure was bigger than Moorland. A whole row of stores faced the railroad depot, and that was only part of the business section. Al Roots said the town was founded in 1882, before statehood. Many of the buildings were new because a fire ten years earlier had wiped out much of the town. Homes, businesses, and even the courthouse had been rebuilt. They had finally organized a fire department in 1902. He said plans were underway to build a mill in the near future.

Al directed the horses across a wooden bridge over the frozen James River. It was smaller than the Des Moines that flowed through Fort Dodge near Babi's house. After traveling a mile west, parallel to the train tracks, we turned south and began climbing a steep hill out of the river valley. The dray rattled along behind us on the first of many trips to move our furniture and household goods, before the train cars were empty.

Once we were out of the James River Valley, the land looked a lot like Iowa. The farm seemed similar to the one in Iowa, but the house was smaller than our other farmhouse. There was a barn and a few outbuildings, and Cottonwood Creek ran to the south. Al Roots pointed out the few trees planted along the north border of the property.

After living in the large boarding house, it took some time to get used to a regular-sized house. Inside the door, narrow steps led down to the basement and up to the first floor. The kitchen was tiny, dominated by the cook stove, but the dining room and parlor stretched the length of the house. At the boarding house, we had a grand stairway with a wooden banister, but this one had tight little steps that twisted and turned.

Carrie and I shared one of the two bedrooms upstairs, and our brothers had the other. Mother and Al Roots took the downstairs bedroom. We were glad to have our own room again and very surprised when, as we explored it, Mother exclaimed, "Oh, this is a charming room." She liked the sloped walls and tall dormer window. "We'll fix it up real cute with a new quilt and curtains!" Again, I wondered who this sweet and kind woman was.

The school was a mile south of the farm. Mother expected Carrie, Edwin, and Bill to begin school the following Monday, but as it turned out, a blizzard hit and we did not leave home for several days. I was way beyond attending school. The next month I would turn sixteen. I had lost four years of schooling, so there was no question about whether I would enroll.

The farm, known as the Thompson farm although Mother purchased it from Michael and Annie McMahon, was on the main road leading to town. In the coming weeks, every neighbor stopped by to say howdy. Each one brought gifts—chokecherry jelly and fresh baked buns, eggs and cream, a sponge cake, and offers of neighborly help. We felt very welcome in our new community.

One girl told Carrie that as soon as we arrived, the party line began ringing with the news, "The newcomers are here! The newcomers are here, and they have five kids!" Every time she told that story, she pursed her lips, as if she needed to hold in her pleasure. I was thrilled by the story *and* that we had a phone, even if we shared the line with a dozen families.

The kindness the neighbors showed soaked into me like the warmth of a glowing hot stove on a bitter cold night. I suddenly realized how cut off we were from our farm and town neighbors in Iowa. With the Spirek family living miles from Moorland, we had not seen much of them either in the last four years.

When asked about ourselves, the rest of us took our cues from Mother and hid the deep secrets of our past. We told our new neighbors we were from Fort Dodge, although we had never lived in Fort Dodge. Our father was "gone," implying that he had died. They knew Mother ran a boarding house in Moorland and that Al Roots was our stepfather. That was all they needed to know, Mother said. My wish was coming true. We were starting fresh.

I suppose our new neighbors were glad to have our big, busy family in Cottonwood Township. They accepted us as we were, and we fit right into the community. Maybe that was because they were just good folks, or maybe they did not want us to look into their pasts too much either. Whatever the reason, I never forgot how important that second chance was to our family. It reminded me of the kindness of my aunt Annie during the darkest time of my life.

<h1 style="text-align:center">19</h1>

April 1904

When you think back on life, a few moments stand out like a light against a dark sky. One of those was my sixteenth birthday in April 1904. I knew something was in the air a few days earlier when a neighbor stopped by. Before she left, she asked if we would be around the coming Saturday. The next day another neighbor, with a twinkle in his eye, said he would not be surprised if we got company that weekend.

Well, about five o'clock on my birthday, buggies started pulling into the yard. Six or eight families from the area came over to welcome us to the community. They brought all kinds of food, sliced ham and beef, scalloped potatoes, apple cobbler, and a Norwegian bread called lefse. Someone made me an angel food cake with thick white frosting. Oh, that was good. Mother put on a big pot of coffee and got every plate out of our cupboard.

After everyone had eaten, the men cleared the furniture out. Someone brought a violin, and another person chorded the piano we brought from Iowa. Eddie eagerly grabbed his horn and joined the fun. The house filled with laughter and the thump of dancing shoes hitting the floor as a neighbor mopped his brow and called out the square dance steps. I eagerly whirled through the steps to these new dances, enjoying the tinkling of the piano keys as the fiddle talked its own language.

I could hardly believe it. In fact, at one point I sneaked off to the outhouse alone, just to collect my thoughts. While it seemed that those big, noisy family gatherings in Iowa were gone forever, here we were with a whole new bunch of people making music and enjoying food and fellowship. It confirmed in my heart that I should never give up hope for tomorrow. Even with deep sorrow, something good could happen just around the corner.

April 1904

Dear Babi,

Thank you for your letter and the gift of money. I plan to save it for something special.

Yes, we had a safe trip. A blizzard began right after we got here, and we've had some long days settling in. The farm needs more work than Al Roots thought. (It had a blanket of snow on it when he came to look at it.) The house is a small two-story. It is in decent shape. Mother is making a lavender quilt and new curtains for the room Carrie and I share.

Please do not worry about us. The nicest things are happening. The whole neighborhood came to our farm on my birthday! They even brought a cake and presents. What a way to turn sixteen. We feel very welcome here.

Thank you again.

I am forever your granddaughter,
Bessie Kloubec

Our family talked about that party for years. I had never had a party before, let alone received a pile of gifts. They brought combs, stockings, a shawl, and things for my hope chest, since I was now of marrying age. I put the embroidered pillowcases, dishtowels, doilies, and oven mitts in a dresser drawer and treasured them, although I never expected to use them. After watching my parents struggle, I preferred the life of an old maid.

20

September 1904

At fourteen, Carrie still struggled to let go of the past and accept our new life. I knew Carrie like I knew my own soul. We always went to the box suppers and even the literary circle, and I knew she wanted to laugh and carry on about nothing with the other girls. But just when a conversation warmed up, she turned away. Something held her back.

One day she disappeared and was gone so long, Mother finally had me saddle up and go look for her. Our new farm dog, Flo, went with me. In fact, she began trotting off to the north, sniffing the ground every so often, so I followed her. We came to the edge of the hill overlooking LaMoure, and I saw Carrie sitting on a fallen log.

I was about to scold her for disappearing, when I saw her hanky all wadded up in her fist and tears streaking down her face. My heart sank. Flo ran ahead of me and nuzzled Carrie.

"Hi, Flo," Carrie said, burrowing her face into the dog's brown fur as if she was her only friend. I dropped the reins and let the horse wander off to pull at the tall grass. I sat down and waited for Carrie to speak, much like we had done with our girl cousins so long ago.

"I miss my cousins and aunts and Babi. I miss Iowa. I miss Joe. I…I miss Father," she choked out as new tears formed and sheeted down her face. "We'll never see them again." Her shoulders quivered with emotion. I sat silently listening to her.

"'Tis nice here. The school is good, and the neighbors are friendly. The other girls are nice. Our house is cozy, and it isn't a boarding house! And even Al Roots seems okay. But then I think about Father and Joe, and I know I do not deserve to be happy. They do not have all the good things we have here. That's my cross to bear."

"Your cross to bear?"

"Yes. My cross is that I cannot be happy knowing they are back in Iowa suffering. It would not be right to feel happy. I will bear their sadness with them." With that, the tears started again.

We sat silently looking at the valley before us, and I prayed for the right words to say to help her. After a while I asked, "Do you think Father wants you to feel sad?"

Carrie looked sideways at me. "Maybe."

"What about Joe?" I ventured. "Do you think he's hoping you're sad?"

"Maybe," she said, stubbornly kicking at the prairie grass.

"Okay, one last question. Do you think your being sad helps them?"

Carrie's head hung down, hiding her eyes.

"I don't want to be sad," she explained. "It's more like I don't deserve to be happy when they aren't. None of us should be enjoying life. Mother shouldn't be giggling with Al Roots, and none of us should ever forget that we left them behind."

I stayed with her for a long while as she talked, but I did not have much advice because I still carried my own cross of guilt and shame. Finally, as dusk set in, we got on the horse and rode double back to the farm, Flo trotting along beside us.

The next day, I went exploring along Cottonwood Creek by myself. Where Hardin Creek in Iowa was a straight little ditch, Cottonwood Creek zigzagged across the prairie like a fly buzzing around a window. A few miles east of our farm, the creek emptied into the James River, known locally as the "Jim."

After the long hours and drudgery at the boarding house, I welcomed having more freedom. Sometimes I took Mother's riding horse and followed the little stream west to where it formed a pool where people fished or swam. Then I would follow it through the prairie to a marshy field of cattails two miles west of us.

On summer evenings, I enjoyed strolling along the creek, letting its freedom and peace soak into my heart. I would poke around, looking for frogs and turtles. Sometimes a critter, perhaps a mink, rabbit, or badger scurried through the grass, which is why I carried a walking stick. Prairie chickens, pheasants, grouse, ducks, and geese nested near the creek. Bullheads jumped from the water, as if they wanted to get a look at me.

I found a special place to sit and listen to the water bubbling along like I had at Hardin Creek. Staring into the opaque green liquid, I tried to see what was beneath the surface. Sometimes a fish sailed by or a dragonfly skimmed the water looking for dinner, but otherwise, life under water remained a mystery.

It was while sitting by the creek that I opened up the dark closet door in my heart and took out the ugly things I stored there. Guilt. Shame. Anger. Resentment. They were like dandelions that sent down roots and continued to grow.

From the time I learned to walk, I had taken care of Joe. It was a much different job than watching my other brothers who grew more independent each day. Joe frustrated me so that sometimes I pounded my pillow at night after a day of supervising him. Could I admit it? I was relieved to let the good people at the Iowa State Home for Feebleminded Children take Joe. I knew it was wrong to feel that way, and I could picture a big sign over my head that said "Bad Sister! Guilty!"

Fear of my father had led me to resent him deeply, and I knew that hatred had no place in a good girl's thoughts or feelings. Still, vivid pictures of the yelling, swearing, pushing, shoving, and punching flashed in front of my eyes. I saw chairs tipped over, heard doors slammed. I hated that time in our lives and hated Father for making me feel like a mouse being tortured by a cat.

My handgun remained tucked away in my room, even though Father was hundreds of miles away. It represented safety, in case he found us way out here. Carrie's mourning for Joe and Father only increased my guilt and self-loathing. What kind of an evil heart did I have anyway? I longed to be like Aunt Annie, who had often comforted me. She loved me when I was the most unlovable, when my face was red and swollen with tears, my hair stringy with sweat, and my voice whiny with fear.

Aunt Annie's love was like sunshine. I wanted to be like her and not the hateful person I was. One thing was for certain: just looking on the good side was not enough to change my dark heart. I decided to write to her.

September 1904

Dear Aunt Annie,

We are fine and getting settled in North Dakota. Homesteaders are still arriving in parts of the state, but people settled the land in our county over twenty years ago. We have a telephone and other modern things. We have fine neighbors. The boys are begging for a bicycle so they can ride to town.

The farm is shaping up, with no small amount of effort. We even missed spring planting because so much work had to be done. Mother and Mr. Roots did not foresee how to handle so many acres.

I fondly remember all the good times we had with our Spirek family. Oh, how I miss you! If we could talk today, I would ask you how to find true peace in my heart. Having peace and joy (and kindness) like you, is my goal.

Please greet everyone for me.

Your niece,
Bessie Kloubec

Oh, how I burned to confess to her the awful feelings I had for Father and Joe, but my courage failed me. Instead, I hoped she would read between the lines and help me somehow. It never occurred to me to ask Mother for help with any of this. Instead, I smiled and followed her orders, playing the part of the perfect daughter.

A letter from Aunt Annie arrived a few weeks later, and I escaped to the creek to read it, flopping down by the creek in the bright sunlight. She reminded me that I had a reputation in the family for being "Brave Bessie." It made me wonder if they still talked about me rushing to Mother's aid in the middle of the night or the day I shot off the gun. She went on to say, "*I pray you will always have the peace of God in your heart. In my own life, I find the key to peace is forgiving others and forgiving myself.*"

When I came to the part about forgiveness, I could not help but gasp because she seemed to know about the dark state of my heart. Maybe Aunt Annie had the key for my predicament. But how could I forgive them? How could I forgive my own wretched self?

I looked over my shoulder to make sure no one was around, but I was alone with the dried brown grass blowing in the breeze and God up in heaven. I looked into the creek and imagined my father's face there, and I began to speak to him.

"I needed you, but you chose alcohol over me," I said out loud, and my voice seemed to boom against the prairie. "That hurt a lot, and it still hurts." I was shouting now as tears rolled down my face. I gripped my knees and rocked back and forth before continuing in a quieter voice. "Father, I forgive you for all the things you did and didn't do."

For a few moments, the world seemed especially still. Father's face disappeared from the water, and Joe's image developed. I sighed and began again. "And Joe, I forgive you for…for being you." I felt so foolish that I looked around again to make sure no one else was near.

Glancing in the water, Joe's face was gone, but my own looked back at me. My tears stopped, and I looked at myself with contempt before going on. "And I forgive you, Bessie, for being a bad daughter and sister. I am sorry to be angry all the time. And I ask God in heaven to forgive it all too."

Admitting my sins to God felt like I had handed my dirtiest laundry to a king and asked him to wash it for me. However, I was desperate to find peace. It was only then that I remembered the prayer we said so long ago in Iowa. "Forgive us our debts as we forgive our debtors." It made me pause. I had said that prayer so many times, but until that moment, the importance of forgiving had been hidden. *When we forgive, are we, in turn, forgiven?* I thought with wonder.

Lying back on the grass, I looked at the sky. Big puffy white clouds drifted across my field of vision, and I watched them, entranced by the bigness of the sky. I drifted off to a peaceful sleep then and awoke refreshed and thinking about my prayer. Was forgiveness the answer? I surely hoped so.

21

October 1904

Time sped by. Although they had not planted a crop, Mother had over an acre of land plowed up for a garden that first year. She spent endless hours ordering seed, planting, and tending to her patch. She had the surprising idea of planting peanuts since the soil looked right for the legume, and the plants came up and did well. She took countless people back to the plot to show off her peanuts. Then on August 16, we had a freeze. Many of the other vegetables slowly recovered from the cold, but that was the end of the peanuts.

She ordered apricot seedlings and planted the tiny trees near the north property line, along with chokecherry roots donated by a neighbor. She also planted a spirea bush on the southwest corner of the house. I could hardly wait for it to bloom the next spring.

The zinnias, marigolds, and hollyhocks had grown so prettily around the foundation of the boarding house and along the path to the little barn and the outhouse in Moorland. When we moved, I tucked the harvested seeds in the trunk. Now they bloomed along the stucco foundation of our new home.

We went about doing many of the things I remembered from our farm in Iowa. My brothers spent a lot of time mending broken fences.

As I said, that first year, we did not plant crops. Looking back, I can see that Mother had complete faith in Al Roots and trusted him to take the lead on farming. She must have been relieved to share with him the burden of caring for our family. However, he was not at the farm that much. He visited the neighbors or went into town. He attended a lot of auctions with the intent of buying up used farm equipment. Soon it was June and past planting time.

When Mother realized we would have to live another whole year on her savings, the sweetness between them began to disappear. When the spring of 1905 arrived, she marshaled the whole family like a general sending troops to war. We went to the fields and planted wheat, rye, and barley. Al Roots helped, but more than once, it was because she stopped him as he headed for town. The tension between them was thicker than sour cream.

I began to see samples of the mother I had known in the past, the one who could give you one look and you would obey. The one you never questioned, never sassed, and with whom you would never share a tender thought. If you did, she might kick you like a mule in the tender belly of your feelings.

Mother's battles with Al Roots differed from those she had had with Father. This time, the rest of us were just casualties in the family war, and not the victims of abuse. I was strangely relieved to see Mother fall back into her blustery old ways again and was thankful that she was not afraid of Al as she was of Father.

I did not blame her for being crabby. Al Roots was such a genial fellow, and it was only when you began putting facts together that a chill poured through you. The fact was he had talked Mother into moving far away from her family. Neither could she complain to her family because they liked Al. Besides, they all believed once you make your bed, you lie in it.

Another fact was, Al never seemed to have any money when it was needed, which meant Mother bought the property, every animal, every piece of equipment, and all the clothing and food for our household. Al always seemed to have more business in town than at home. Except for what George and I earned by hiring out, it was Mother's money that got us through to the fall of 1905 when we sold our first crop.

To others we probably seemed like a normal, happy family, though surely the neighbors commented to each other about Al Roots not getting the crop in that first spring. Still, we had become part of the community. George made friends in LaMoure right away and went to town every weekend. Sometimes he took Carrie and me along. There were many young people in the area, and someone always cooked up a way to get together and have fun.

In winter, they held skating parties, with a dozen or more young people sailing around on the frozen river. Afterward, we would go to someone's house to warm up and gab over hot chocolate. In the summer, baseball dominated the good times. The teams were made up of men and boys. Carrie and I always played ball back in Iowa, so it seemed strange to sit and watch the games. I did not care to sit on the rough wooden stands as a spectator, but Carrie loved baseball, whether she played or watched the game.

Every few weeks, there was a dance at the town hall in LaMoure or a show at the opera house. Carrie and I always begged to go along to town with George. I loved to dance. Songs like "A Bird in a Gilded Cage" or "Who Threw the Overalls in Mrs. Murphy's Chowder" made it hard to sit in my chair as my feet kept tapping. The truth is I hardly ever sat out a dance.

Carrie did not like dancing much. She complained that if she did not have two left feet, her partners did. I was glad she came along, though, because if some fellow started pestering me too much, Carrie would just frown at them and purse her lips. Even though she was two years younger than I was, no one wanted to tangle with her. George, of course, was my best defender, but he tended to pay more attention to other girls than to his sisters. Overall, these activities made life enjoyable.

22

May 1905

In 1905, the neighbors invited us to attend Cottonwood Presbyterian Church. They had begun meeting at the schoolhouse a couple of months earlier.

We had not been to church in years, but how could we turn down such an invitation when the whole neighborhood had been so welcoming to us? Mother said yes right away, but when I looked into her eyes, I saw fear and shame. I thought of our past experience with a church.

Carrie had a conniption about this. "Cottonwood Church is *Protestant*!" she sputtered. "We're not supposed to go to a Protestant church. We could be condemned to hell! What if we're struck by lightning?" On and on she went. The more she talked, the more determined I was to go to church and live to tell about it. Our neighbors seemed like good people. Would God really condemn them to eternal hell because they went to the wrong church? Mother did not think so either.

One Sunday in May, we put on our best clothes, got in the wagon, and headed down the road to church. When Al Roots decided at the last minute that he did not want to go, I could see Mother falter for a moment, but she decided to go without him.

Cottonwood Church and our church in Fort Dodge were as different as ginger ale and cod liver oil. In Fort Dodge, the voice of the priest echoed inside the tall, stately brick building. The air was solemn and worshipful. Everyone sat, stood, and kneeled in unison. An organ swept the congregation up in a grandeur that went far beyond our daily lives. I did not understand the priest as he stood with his back to us, praying in Latin to God on our behalf. What I did understand was that God was very big and I was very small.

That Sunday was a lovely spring day. As we entered the schoolhouse, the windows were open, and the room was bright with sunlight. People laughed and talked. Most of them had attended Sunday school the hour before and were taking a short break before the service. We took seats near the back, and an usher passed out hymnals. I squeezed my hanky uneasily until my knuckles turned white. Carrie stared straight ahead. Mother tapped her chin. The boys fidgeted.

The pastor welcomed us all, said a prayer, and quoted from the Bible. Then everyone began to sing, "What a friend we have in Jesus, all our sins and griefs to bear! What a privilege to carry everything to God in prayer..."

It stirred in me the memory from the fall before, when I had poured out my heart to God about my anger. Suddenly I realized a change had happened in me. The old anger was gone! I had not even noticed it disappear, kind of like when a sore thumb heals up and you forget about it. At that moment, the path to God seemed as simple as giving him my sins and griefs, and I had plenty. What a friend I'd found in Jesus!

I glanced around and saw that Carrie wore a look of wonder on her face. Beyond her, Mother smiled, and Eddie sang out strong and clear. George and Bill even sang along. We had found happiness in church, of all places. That day cemented something for us. Another church had opened its door to our family, and we had walked through it. We became regular attenders at Cottonwood.

May 1905

Dear Aunt Annie,

In your letter last fall, you offered some advice. I took your words seriously, and I am happy to report how much you helped me. I had a lot of forgiving to do, especially forgiving myself over things. I feel like a new person. Thank you so much.

We are doing fine. We started to attend a new church that meets at the school. Have you heard the song "What a Friend We Have in Jesus"? It says what I have found to be true. I ordered the sheet music and plan to send you a copy when it arrives.

The men are planting the crops, wheat, barley, and rye. Hope you are all well. Please say hello to everyone for me. The hardest part of being here is we miss all of you. Let me know if you have any more advice.

Love,
Your niece Bessie

In time, I had a chance to talk with Carrie again about the cross she felt she must bear. This time, however, I knew what to say to her.

23

April 1906

In 1906 when I turned eighteen, Mother surprised me with a small buggy and a Morgan horse. Land's sake, a buggy and a horse of my own! I suspected the special gift was some kind of payment for years of slaving away at the farm and later the boarding house. While Carrie and the younger boys went to school, George and I were obligated to help the family. Failing to finish sixth grade was something I was ashamed to admit to our new friends in North Dakota.

I named the horse Bump after our first bumpy ride. Every day I hitched up the rig and went some place. When someone asked me to work for them for a few days, I was eager to provide my own transportation.

That summer, I drove the ten miles to the park at Grand Rapids almost every Sunday. Carrie or friends from town often went along. It was an ideal spot for a picnic. The Jim flowed all around it, almost making it into an island. Flowers bloomed everywhere.

We played like children on the sky-high slide and teeter-totter, screaming and laughing all the while. My favorites were the swings with their squeaky chains. Sometimes a band played or we watched a baseball game and recalled the good old days of Billy Sunday. The daring ones went swimming in the river, but wading into the cool muddy water never appealed to me.

Truly, that horse and buggy were a turning point in my life. I sure turned heads when I went flying up the road driving a rig with a big black horse. Oh, Bump was a beauty, with a white streak down his face and four stocking feet. He had a mind of his own, but I managed to keep control of him most of the time. I kept my black buggy shined up too. It is possible I neglected some of my duties around the house because of it, but Mother never said a word.

My spirits turned too. I learned that forgiving once was not enough. I tried each day to go through a forgiveness list. As I did that, the darkness of the past years drifted further away, and the familiar rock in the pit of my stomach left completely. Carrie had also come to terms with her guilt, although she still kept Father and Joe close in her heart.

Bump helped bring out the playful side of me that had disappeared when I was eleven. Now I was eighteen and enjoying my life. When I went to a dance, my feet moved as fast as ever, but my smile was more genuine. Sometimes I could not help myself; I would have to sing out a song that was going through my mind.

My life was getting happier, but Mother's was not. She worried all the time. She had worked hard and staked everything on the farm, just to find out her new husband liked to gad about more than work. I myself had heard he liked to play cards in town.

In the spring of 1905 and again in 1906, she was the one who sat at the table and figured out what seed to buy and what equipment we needed. She ordered and paid for everything. She was the one who mustered us out of bed at dawn during planting and harvest seasons. Carrie and I cooked a hardy breakfast and packed lunches each morning, while the boys did the barn chores. Then we all headed for the fields. George and Al Roots took turns plowing the land with the team. Then we would walk behind the plow to plant the seed and cover it.

I could not help comparing Al Roots to my own father. When he was sober, Father was a hard worker and a skilled laborer. Oh, Al Roots could do things, but never like Father. Al might fix some fence, but he would spend twice as much time telling the neighbors what a good job he had done. Because he had plenty of charm, we overlooked his flaws for the most part. He still got along well with the boys, but sometimes Carrie and I poked fun at his bragging.

Once the seed came up, Al Roots went out to the fields every day to measure the plants. He constantly watched the weather. Would it rain or hail? At night, he would sit at the dining room table figuring how much money the crops would bring in. Of course, he spent ample time in town discussing market prices.

Our family had another big change the summer of 1906. Carrie, who was sixteen, moved to Valley City to attend summer school. The state was desperate for teachers in the country schools that populated every township. Cottonwood Township alone had three schools, so we pooled our money and sent her to the six weeks of training for a teacher's certificate. She took the train to Valley City and stayed in the dormitory. She only came home one time that summer, for the Fourth of July.

> *Dear Bessie,*
>
> *I am so homesick. I have twenty days left. School is pretty easy. Moreover, it is something else to live in this big brick building. Valley City is at least as big as Fort Dodge. Guess I am a "city girl" now. The other students are okay. Mostly they are homesick too.*
>
> *How are things going on the farm? I hope you got rain and not a frost like the first summer we were in Dakota. Box Bill's ears for me and tell Eddie he had better be able to play a new tune for me when I get home or else!*
>
> *Any news from Iowa? Do you ever think about going back?*
>
> *Love,*
> *Carrie*

It was hard to believe we were sisters. Here she was in teacher's training and longing to go back to Iowa. I had no desire to be a teacher or to see Iowa again, although something was stirring in me.

That fall, Carrie took a job at Cottonwood Township No. 3, four miles from the farm. They had a hard time finding a teacher because the families would not or could not board the teacher. Carrie lived close enough to ride over each day. In September, she began saddling up old Billy each morning and heading off to work.

My little sister was a schoolteacher. Her life was moving on, but mine seemed stuck. Stuck and safe. Even if I wanted a change, I wasn't sure what I would do. Or if anything was worth the risk.

24

October 1906

I was hanging wash on the line one windy morning in the fall of 1906 when a stranger galloped by on a chestnut mare. His hair was the color of a new copper penny, and his wide-brimmed hat flopped on his back, tethered by a leather chin string that kept it from blowing into the ditch. He had a rifle tied to the side of the saddle. As I stood there, a clothespin between my teeth as I threw a sheet over the clothesline, I wondered who the fellow was. That was my first look at Gale Muir.

We, of course, knew John and Lena Muir who lived in LaMoure. We often saw their kids, Grace, Maude, John, Jr., Vera, Ruth, and Vernon, at parties or dances or up at Grand Rapids Park. John made land deals in the county and was part owner in the new grain elevator in LaMoure. Al Roots fancied himself a friend of John's, but I never thought they quite belonged in the same circle. Rumor had it that John had sold a farm a few miles southwest of us to his parents.

A couple of hours later, a train of wagons and drays trailed south past our farm. We were at the dinner table when we heard a rumble and went out to watch the arrival. I noticed John Muir riding next to the fellow with the red hair. He pulled away from the wagons and swung into our yard to let us know his parents, Robert and Mary Muir, were moving into the neighborhood, along with his youngest brother, Gale.

I did not think much about it at the time. There were a lot of young men in the neighborhood and many more across the county.

I loved to do a polka or waltz with a boy, but that was where my interest in boys ended. If I ever got married, my husband had to meet several conditions, such as there would be no drinking. I detested fast talkers like Al Roots. Neither did I want a husband who left to work in faraway places, like those railroad men that lived at the boarding house. That eliminated quite a lot of the boys around LaMoure.

Some boys were already out behind the dance hall tipping a few on weekends. One boy asked if I would wait for him while he went away to college. Sit home every weekend wondering what he was doing? Not a chance. My favorite bad experience with a boy was the time a fellow rode with me to Grand Rapids Park one Sunday. He stuck me with the bill for his ice cream cone. That was the last time I gave him a ride!

My Spirek uncles, Uncle Anton and Uncle Charles, served as examples of what a husband should be. They knew how to show kindness to their wives and children and worked hard to support their families, but they also knew how to have fun.

Al Roots was no example at all. The fact that he always wanted Carrie and me to sit on his knee made him even more repulsive. Something about it just did not seem right. As for Father, well, he had almost ruined any thoughts I ever had about getting married. How could you trust what a man might become in five years or ten? What if I chose someone that changed as much as he did? It all brought me back to the question of how could you know whether you were making the right choice? That is why I did not spend much time thinking about boys or men or marriage. Not much time at all.

25

Robert Muir rode to our place a few days after they moved in and talked to Mother about hiring me. He asked Mother about hiring me to do housework, because Mrs. Muir suffered with arthritis. Mother saw an opportunity for a little extra income, so she assured him I was able to run a household.

The next day, I rigged up my buggy before sunup and left for the Muir place. Once there, I unhitched the buggy and led Bump into the corral.

Robert and Mary Muir's two-story white house stood back from the road, beyond a small woods. The tidy yard looked like one in a storybook, with a red barn, grain bins, and a rope swing hanging from a tree in the yard. The place had a settled feel to it, as if it had been there forever. I had been to the farm before they bought the property, but I had never been inside the house.

That morning, I walked to the kitchen door and let myself into the house. I lit a fire in the stove and went back out to pump a pail full of water. After dipping some into the enamel coffee pot on the range, I went foraging for food. There were only basic items in the pantry.

I took a lamp and carefully opened the door to the root cellar. The steps were steep and narrow, and the space at the bottom was all but empty. We had lined our own basement shelves with canned goods. We also had a twenty-gallon crock of carrots, a smaller one with sauerkraut, a bin full of potatoes, gunnysacks full of onions, and a bushel basket of squash. The Muir's cellar held a table with an egg crate and a pitcher of milk on it.

I was back in the kitchen stirring up pancakes and scrambled eggs when Robert Muir came downstairs. He seemed surprised and happy to see me. "Well Bessie, you're a right early riser!" he said as he sat down in a captain's chair located where the early morning sunrays could warm him. I smiled and stirred the batter.

He was quite a man in size and looks. Piercing pale blue eyes looked out from shaggy brows. He must have been six feet tall and had rich red hair, with a long beard the same color. I had heard he was highly respected in Jackson, Minnesota, where they came from.

"Tell me," he said in a gravelly voice, "are you really from Fort Dodge?" I nodded my head. Tongue-tied, that is what I was.

"That's straight south of Jackson," he said. "We were practically neighbors!"

"We moved here in the spring of 1904. 'Tis a long train ride," I said once I found my voice. I poured pancake batter in the frying pan and flipped the pancakes as they began bubbling. Once the pancakes were fried and on a plate on the warming shelf, I dumped some coffee grounds in the pot. A memory of the first time I made coffee at age eleven with my father sitting at the kitchen table flitted through my mind. I poured the eggs into a second cast-iron pan.

"So hit is a long trail out here. Tell me, are the winters harder here than in Iowa?" His Scottish brogue surprised me.

"Yes, sir. Colder. You can hardly stay warm, no matter what you do. We've had a lot of snow too." My eyes glanced toward the cellar door. "If you don't mind my saying so, you'll need to get in a winter supply of food and pile up plenty of coal and wood near the house."

"Well, that's good advice, Bessie. We are going to fill up the larder! My son, John, painted a pretty picture of LaMoure County, but he did not say much about the winters. But, lassie, I was born in Upper Canada, where hit got very cold."

Just then, Mrs. Muir came slowly into the room, and he stood. The top of her head only came up to his chin. Even with her health problems, she had pulled her thin hair into a bun and looked as neat as ironed lace. She had a full chin and cheeks, and her light blue eyes were lively. She smiled and gave me a nod, which I hoped was approval for taking over her kitchen.

I curtsied and said, "Good morning, Mrs. Muir." I had never curtsied to anyone in my life, so then I blushed. However, it somehow seemed right because I was in awe of Robert and Mary Muir right from the beginning.

Mary Muir's mannerisms reminded me of Babi, and I had to blink tears from my eyes. She walked stiffly, but her back remained erect, and that gave her a stately air. She and Babi both seemed to hold back their power, as if they were holding back the reins on a horse able to gallop a thousand miles. Still, before I knew it, I was chatting away as we ate breakfast at the kitchen table.

"Bessie is from Fort Dodge, so we didn't live so far apart before we moved here," Robert Muir told his wife between bites. "Lass," he said, waving his fork at me. "Why don't you tell us about your family? Are they all here at LaMoure?"

"Just my nearest of kin. Mother and my sister Carrie. My brothers, George, Edwin, and Bill. And my stepfather, Al Roots. You've maybe met some of them." My heart pinged as a picture of Joe passed through my head. I need not mention him, as he did not live here. "The rest of the relatives are in the Fort Dodge area."

"And your father?"

I looked down. "He's gone," I said smoothly. That was the truth.

"I'm sorry to hear that, Bessie."

"Thank you," I said as I studied the plate in front of me.

"How did you happen to come to LaMoure?"

I frowned a moment and shrugged. "Mother was running a boarding house at Moorland when she met Al Roots. I guess 'twas his idea to come out here. They got married in '03, and we came out the next spring." I did not say Al Roots had not even gotten a crop in the first year. I suspected that Robert Muir would not have let that happen.

"We had thirteen children," he said. "We've lost three, God rest their souls." He paused for a moment and then seemed to will himself onward. "You probably know our daughter, Kate, and her husband, Arthur Raub. They moved here in August, and we will have more family living in North Dakota before too long. 'Tis a Muir invasion!

"Back in Jackson, we have brothers and sisters and kids and grandkids, but John is a good salesman. He convinced us that coming here was worth pulling up roots. Good thing Gale will be here to do the hard work," he said. He leaned back in his chair, his breakfast plate emptied. He took out a plug of tobacco and stuck it in his mouth.

I looked around for any sign of this Gale.

As if reading my thoughts, Mary Muir said, "Gale went back to Minnesota to help some of the others move out here. And to see his fiancé." She seemed to study me extra close. "I'm glad you're going to help us, Bessie. I'm not feeling as up to this big adventure as I should."

"You said you were born in Upper Canada?' I asked them.

"Aye, lass," Robert Muir responded. "Our parents left Scotland in the 1820s, inspired by free land. Later they moved near the United States border in Ontario. That's where I met my 'Highland Mary.'" He squeezed his wife's hand, and she blushed a bit. "After we got married, we came to Minnesota with my brother, Andrew, and my sister, Mary, and their families. Anyway, hit was a rough time. We homesteaded a quarter of land."

Mary Muir again smiled with her eyes. "My Bobby felled the trees and split them and built us a little cabin. We lived there for twenty-five years. When we outgrew it, he added on a new big section." She paused a moment and then went on. "We moved into Jackson to live the retired life two years ago, but here we are starting all over again."

"Bessie, if we're going to be talk'n while you're work'n, would you be so kind as to bring my knitting basket in here?" Mary Muir asked. I liked the long, narrow kitchen best because it let in so much bright morning sunlight. I was intrigued by the two stairways to the basement, one from the kitchen and one from a lean-to.

Her delicate lace curtains already covered the tall windows in the living room. A coal stove stood in the middle of the room, warming an assortment of easy chairs and rockers. A large dining room table stood at one end, and a small reading table was in front of a window. None of the furniture matched like our red velveteen sofa and chairs, but the room seemed homey and peaceful.

As I went into the living room in search of the basket, I realized how full my heart was. I already loved these people, though I hardly knew them. It seemed like something special was happening. After settling Mrs. Muir in the kitchen rocker, I put the teakettle on to heat. I whisked the dishes to a dishpan on the counter and shaved some soap into the water. All the while, we were talking easy, like old friends with a lot to catch up on.

That afternoon, I unpacked Mary Muir's good dishes. I washed them carefully and placed them in the sideboard. She rested for a while but then sat near where I worked and talked about all the family meals served on those dishes. We shared a common interest in sewing too.

Being at the Muirs' hardly seemed like work. Before I knew it, the clock said it was time to go home. At the end of the day, I slipped a Johnny Cake into the oven, and Mr. Muir paid me a day's wages.

"I pay as I go," he said. "No reason to be owe'n anyone. The good Lord takes care of us when we act uprightly." I thanked him and—I could not help myself—gave him a hug and then threw my arms around Mary Muir.

On the way home, Bump seemed to absolutely prance. "What's got into you?" I asked my dear horse. "Did you have a good day with the horses at the Muir farm?" My own spirits were higher than a flag on the Fourth of July. I stopped the buggy by our back door and ran into the house, excited to tell about my day.

Just as I rushed up the steps into the kitchen, a metal pie pan flew by my head. I leaned to the side as it whizzed past me and clattered down the steps.

"Do you think I'm a fool?" Mother shouted at Al Roots. She stood with her eyes narrowed and her hands on her hips. Al stood with his hands at his side, a silly look on his face. The tension in the air was as thick as rice pudding. She began reaching behind her for another pie plate.

"Now, Mary, be reasonable. You're acting like a crazy woman!" The second pie plate sailed toward Al, who caught it.

"This is only half the money we should get for the crop!" Mother shouted at the top of her lungs. It was only then that I noticed a wad of money in her left fist. "Do you think I do not know how much grain was in that wagon? Do you think I do not know the price of barley? Where is the rest of the money?"

"That is all there is, Mary." I could not decipher the funny look on Al's face. "Be reasonable," he continued in a soothing voice. "Sometimes I wonder about you, Mary. Are you getting touched in the head?" Al was slipping backward toward me. He squeezed past me down the stairs.

"I expect to see the bill of sale! You better find it by tomorrow!" Mother leaned forward as she shouted, as though she wanted to catch up with him, but her feet would not move. He went out the door.

Mother looked at me, and I studied her. Accusing Mother of being crazy was a very low blow. Many of our relatives in Iowa said Father was crazy, and we had had to send our Joe to an institution. Even hinting at mental problems in our family brought a sense of uneasiness. Mother was not crazy. Why, she had always had a temper. That did not make her crazy.

Al was the crazy one, was he not? I glanced out the window and saw him take hold of Bump's harness and coax him toward the barn, as if nothing had happened.

Mother slowly opened her hand to reveal the money she held. "He took the barley to the elevator in town. He says this is all the money he got from selling the whole crop. How can that be?"

I just shook my head and went quietly to my room, relieved to get away from the tension. I was glad the other kids were not there to witness these new troubles. I lay across the bed, taking deep breaths because it seemed like I could not get enough air. My fingers squeezed the soft material in the quilt Mother had made for us. The squares were made of leftover fabric from new dresses or from clothes we had outgrown that still had good fabric in them. The middle squares were all lavender prints. The next rows were all soft greens. The edge was a mix of lavender and green colors.

Fingering the soft quilt helped me calm down a bit. Only minutes ago I'd come home happy as a robin in spring. Now dark storm clouds glowered over me again. I decided not to let this get me down. I would be all right. Thinking about Robert and Mary Muir made me smile and relax a bit more. I took a deep breath and let my mind drift. I thought of their sparse provisions for winter and decided to do something about it. I would take some gifts over to them when I went to work in the morning.

Getting up inspired, I went to the basement and filled a basket with jars of pickles and jellies then filled another with carrots, potatoes, and squash. We had an abundance of food stored away. Even if we did not get much money from the crop, I knew we would have plenty to eat. I took the goods, stashed them in the buggy, and covered them with a horse blanket.

The next morning, Carrie and I went out at dawn and prepared to leave for our jobs. A light fog made the world seem strange. You could see your breath. Bump nickered when he saw me. I stroked his nose and got out his oats. After feeding him, I put the harness on and led him to the shed where I hitched up the buggy. Carrie saddled Billy and rode off to the west, her lunch and teacher's books in her saddlebags.

I clicked at Bump, and we trotted off to the south. It was funny how sounds carried in the early morning. When I got to the little bridge over the creek, I stopped and just listened to the water trickling underneath. The sound was so clear. A fish jumped farther downstream, and the rushes rustled as some animal scurried away. I regretted having to move on, but I was also eager to begin work.

After parking the buggy and unhitching Bump, I carried the baskets into the house and put them on the table, happy to bring such a nice gift.

A few minutes later, Robert Muir appeared. "Bessie! Did you bring this or did an elf stop by?" He was in fine humor. He went to the table and looked over the goods. "Did you help make this jelly? I do believe I might have some with my bread this morning." Then he turned to me with the kindest eyes I had ever seen. "Thank ye, lassie."

I beamed and then turned to begin making breakfast.

"We got a letter from Gale yesterday," Mr. Muir continued. "Hit seems he's delayed in Jackson for a while. I guess I will have to get the farm up and running by myself. But first we'll need to go into

LaMoure and invest in a winter supply of flour, sugar, coffee, and the like."

On the third day of work, I decided to skip the buggy and just saddle up Bump. Carrie had already saddled Billy for her morning ride to the school. It looked easy, but Carrie was bigger than me and Billy was smaller than Bump. Ordinarily, George or Al Roots helped me, but George was working for a neighbor and Al Roots was not out of bed yet. I put the saddle on top of the corral fence, moved Bump next to the fence, and then hoisted the saddle onto his back. After cinching him up, I led him through the gate, closed it, and climbed up the fence and onto Bump's back.

The fourth day, I rode Bump bareback. It was just easier to throw a blanket over his back, put his harness on, climb the fence, and jump on his back and go. I even considered walking, but it was getting late in the fall and I did not want to walk home at the end of the day if the weather turned bad. I rode bareback for several weeks after that, unless I was hauling something. I only used my little buggy on weekends.

We had settled on my duties. I worked for the Muirs three or four days a week. On Mondays, I would do the wash. That was my hardest job. Robert Muir helped me lift the big boiler onto the range to heat the water. I stripped the bedding and scrubbed the sheets on the washboard, wringing them out by hand. The white things and underwear soaked while I hung sheets on the clothesline. Then I scrubbed and wrung out the next batch. After that, it was the colored clothes and finally the heavy work clothes. Robert Muir planned to get a washing machine someday. I was glad Mother had one at home because it sure made things easier.

Wednesdays I baked bread. Fridays I cleaned house. Each day there were other smaller things to do. I might iron or bake a cake. Most days I made breakfast and a hearty noontime dinner. Some weeks I went along into town to help with the shopping or did other jobs, like getting the winter coats out of the trunk to air.

They talked a lot about their youngest son, but I wondered if I would ever get to meet this mysterious Gale.

26

The weeks flew by. Indian summer passed, and each day seemed a little cooler than the last. Now when I left for work, it was pitch-dark out. Mrs. Muir wanted me to stay with them during the week, but I preferred going home at the end of the day. Even though Mother was cranky, I knew it helped to have me around for moral support and to help with the work. Carrie also left early in the morning and arrived home at dusk, but she then had to prepare to teach eight grades the next day, while my evenings were free.

One morning when I opened the door to leave for work, the cold wind swirled around me like a lady's skirt on the dance floor. I was glad I had worn two petticoats to keep warm. I closed the door behind me and picked up my satchel. I had packed my nightie and some extra underwear in case I needed to stay overnight. An east wind blew, signaling a possible storm. Carrie had already left. I hoped she had made arrangements if the weather turned bad.

George was home, and I thought about waking him to give me a ride, but decided I could do it myself. Lying in my nice warm bed, I had been confident I could ride bareback and manage the satchel. Now I was not so sure. I held out the lantern and started down the steps when something made me look up.

The horse and buggy standing in front of the house gave me a start! The buggy's lantern light cast a circle that showed a man sitting on the rig. He turned to me and took his hat off. It was Gale Muir, I was sure, though I did not know he had come back from Minnesota.

He got down from the buggy seat, reached out to shake my hand, and said, "Miss Bessie? I am Gale Muir. Would you like a ride?"

"Why, certainly," I said with a smile. "It's nice to finally meet you, Gale." I put down the satchel and pumped his hand. I put out the lantern and left it on the step while he stashed my satchel behind the seat. I gathered my skirts, and he took my hand and helped me climb up on the seat. The buggy lantern cast a cozy glow around us.

He clucked at the horse, and we jolted forward. Suddenly I felt very shy. Minutes passed by, and neither of us said a word. I looked at him out of the corner of my eye and found that he was looking at me! I quickly turned my head forward again. What to do? What to do? Finally, I found my voice.

"'Twas very nice of your father to ask you to give me a ride."

"Oh, Father didn't send me. He was not even up yet when I left the house. But I heard there was a young lady riding around the country bareback and figured she needed a lift on a wintery day like this."

"In that case, I owe you an even bigger thank you. That was very thoughtful."

All this time, he twirled a little leather rope with one hand and drove with the other. Did he feel nervous around me?

"When did you arrive from Minnesota?"

"Yesterday afternoon. My sister and brother-in-law came with me. Janet and Albert Hunt. They are the newest residents of Cottonwood Township. I am surprised you did not see or hear all the commotion. We had a wagon and two drays. We moved them in late in the afternoon."

I knew the Hunts had purchased a farm two miles south of our farm but had not heard or seen anything of the move.

"You don't say? Our whole family was gone for the afternoon. My sister invited us to her school to watch her students in a special program. Just think, we left for a few hours and a new family moved in just like that."

"Just like that," he repeated. Later I learned they had worked until midnight to unload the drays and put the house in order. The Hunts wanted to stay in their own home their first night in North

Dakota. Gale had done the bulk of the heavy lifting, yet he had gotten up at 5:00 a.m. to give me a ride.

When we got to the Muir farm, he pulled around by the back door to let me off. I stepped down, took my satchel, and looked up at him. "Many thanks," I said gratefully.

"I'm going hunting now," he said. "Yesterday I saw a covey of birds land west of here. I'll get there about the time they're looking for breakfast." He patted a gun stashed behind him. "You might expect to have prairie chicken for supper tonight." He smiled, tipped his hat again, and clucked to the horse.

The rig turned around and vanished into the dark. Only the sound of the horse's hooves and the creak of the rig betrayed the fact that someone was out there. I stood outside the darkened Muir house and wondered if I had just dreamed the whole thing. Maybe I was still in my own bed, but no, the bone-chilling air told me I was awake. And I had met the man with the red hair.

As the morning wore on, ice pellets and later snow began hitting the east window. It looked like a good storm was brewing. Gale was not home yet, and I wondered about Carrie. Would she dismiss school early?

Friday's cleaning was well underway about ten thirty that morning when the phone rang. I glanced at Mary Muir, and she nodded for me to answer it. I stepped up to the mouthpiece and put the handset to my ear.

"Hello?"

"Bessie, is that you?"

"Yes, Mother."

"I called to tell you a storm is coming in and you should hurry back home."

"Oh, I can't do that. Gale Muir gave me a ride this morning, and he hasn't come back from hunting yet."

"Gale Muir. Now why would he be giving you a ride?"

"I don't know. He just did. Anyway, do not worry about me. I brought my satchel in case I needed to stay over."

Mary Muir nodded at me again as she rocked in her chair. It was a real comfort to have a kind employer.

After a few more words with Mother, I hung up. Just then, the kitchen door flew open, and Robert and Gale tromped in, stamping snow off their boots onto the braided rug.

"Look what the storm blew in," Robert Muir said. "And he brought enough game to keep us well fed for some time!"

Indeed, Gale had a gunnysack with four prairie chickens in it. I quickly put a large pot on to boil, so the game could be dressed as soon as possible. Meanwhile, the men went out to bring in a big pail of water and more coal from the lean-to next to the house. When the water was ready, they took the pot and the birds to the lean-to and made quick work of them.

I put aside my house cleaning for the time being. After adding more coal in the stove, I took the large roaster out of the pantry and scrubbed some potatoes. When the birds were ready, I placed them in the roaster, cut onion over them, and used ample salt and pepper. Then I poured a pint of cream over the whole works and slipped the roaster in the oven.

For our noon meal, I warmed up the vegetable soup from earlier in the week and cut thick slices of bread. We sat down at the kitchen table with the oil lamp casting a glow over the table. It was only 12:30 p.m., but the sky had disappeared in a swirl of snow. The wind shrieked, and we could feel the drafts from the doors and windows with each gust.

Mr. Muir blessed the food and we started to eat. Gale sat opposite me, which was a real problem, because I did not know where to look. Whenever I looked up and our eyes met, lightning bolts shot between us. I concentrated on my soup for most of the meal. I did not know which was worse, staring into his pale blue eyes or staring at his red hair. To be honest, I do not even know what we talked about at that meal. The emotions stirring inside me were so strong that everything else seemed to disappear, including the wind.

Later, Mary Muir went to rest. Robert Muir read his Bible by the west window, and Gale left to take care of chores outside. I finished the house cleaning and checked the roasting birds. It was clear I would need to spend the night because the snow was coming fast and furious. The men folk added coal to the stoves in the kitchen and living room every hour just to keep the house warm.

The rest of the day was like a holiday. Dinner came out of the oven about five o'clock, so we ate our big meal then. I was relieved that the roasted birds were quite tasty and tender. Each of the Muirs exclaimed over the creamy, moist meat.

Mary Muir helped me clean up the kitchen. "When we're finished here, you can take your bag up to the blue bedroom," she said quietly. "You can stay in there tonight."

I knew there were three bedrooms upstairs. They slept in the one with green striped wallpaper and heavy wood furniture. Another room had a big bed and dresser with blue flowered wallpaper. The third one had a narrow bed and plain white paint. I had assumed I would sleep in that room or on the sofa downstairs.

"Gale decided to take the room with the little bed. He doesn't like all those flowers on the walls in the big room, I guess," said Mrs. Muir. "Besides, we'll have a lot of company who can use the larger bed."

My face colored a bit as I thought about sleeping there, just down the hall from the big redhead. Would he hear me cough or use the chamber pot or wash my face in the basin next morning? How embarrassing.

When I got back downstairs, the men had set the reading table next to the coal stove in the parlor. "Do you play whist, Bessie?" asked Gale. When I shook my head, he added, "Well, it's easy. We'll teach you."

I put the coffee pot on the kitchen range and sat down to learn the game. Mary Muir and I were partners. I was surprised how quickly the time passed. My shyness faded as I learned to shuffle and deal, trump, and trick. Before long, we were all at ease, laughing and joking as we played the game.

Promptly at seven, Mary Muir turned in for the night. As she slowly made her way up the stairs, the men turned to each other and said, "Widow whist." It was a game we could play with three people. I poured another cup of coffee for each of us, and we played three more games. Afterward we sat at the table, listening to the wind howl around the corner of the house and the crackle of the fire in the pot-bellied stove next to us.

"Roosevelt is doing a good job," Robert Muir said. He rolled his words so the president's named sounded like "Ruu ze velt." "He's a man's man, and he's as wise as he is smart! The more you know, the better you can lead."

The topics went from politics to the recent earthquake in San Francisco. "Well, I feel sorry for all those lost lives," said Robert Muir, "but I'd like to see them survive this storm!"

On new inventions, he said, "Someday we'll be able to listen to music without playing hit ourselves! Yes, sir, the Victrola will open up the world of music to us. We will just turn on a switch and hear Mozart! Aye, there's a new world coming."

He sat twirling his cane as he gave opinions on many topics. Gale had several witty comments. I was surprised how often they matched my own thoughts, though I did not say much. I was beginning to feel more at ease with him, but I still could not bear to look directly at him.

My eyes grew heavy as we talked in the dim light. The roar of the storm seemed to die down a bit. "The eye of the storm!" said Robert Muir, and I jerked awake. "Hit reminds me of 1869 when I spent a night in a snowbank!" That brought me wide awake, and I leaned forward to hear his next tale.

"Thirty-seven years ago this March, I was in Jackson with oxen after a load of wood. I started home just at night," he said. *"When suddenly one of those storms which the country is noted for came up, and by the time I got out of Lee's place, you could not see ten feet ahead. I had faith in the team and believed they would keep to the road, but the storm grew worse, and soon it became impossible not only to see but even to feel."*

Our eyes were glued on the old man. He twirled his cane, lost in the story. He continued, *"I unhitched the oxen, and we started to find the road. But I had to give that up, so I fell in behind the oxen and trusted to luck to bring us somewhere.*

"After we had traveled until I began to give out, I stopped and tried to fasten the oxen with the chain to a snow crust. Then I dug a hole in

the bank and turned in. I hope you never have to do that, Bessie," he said, and stopped and shot some tobacco into a spittoon Mary Muir kept near his chair.

"Soon I heard a movement and, crawling out, discovered the oxen were gone, but as I could not tell which way they had gone, I again sought my downy couch. He-he. I lay down on my back and worked both legs, striving to keep my feet from freezing, until I was nearly used up. When I got outside again, the storm was still doing business, but I could see the moon was just up, so it must have been three o'clock, and back I went under the snow. At daylight I started on again and soon ran into a stake. Then I knew where I was, and starting straight west, I struck the little log house in just a mile. That day, after rest and a good breakfast, I struck out and found the team coming home. They were about two miles southeast of where we camped."

The room was silent except for the wailing of the wind.

"I was twenty-eight years old, and my Highland Mary was waiting in that log cabin for me, along with little Lizzy and baby John. I could hardly die in a snowstorm with them counting on me."

"Yes, sir," Robert Muir concluded, "we're now in the eye of the storm. The wind will soon start to blow from the west, and tomorrow it will blow itself out!"

I smiled at him, amazed that he knew so much about the weather, about everything.

"Lassie, you go to bed. I like to bank the fire and turn off the lamps myself," he said, patting my hand.

I said my goodnights and went upstairs. As sleepy as I was, after I got into my flannel nightie and crawled in the big bed, bigger than the one I shared with Carrie, I could not sleep. I heard the men clump up the stairs and go into their rooms. I heard their boots drop to the floor and imagined them sitting on the edges of their beds, unlacing them. After a while I heard soft snoring. I decided to pray for my family and that Carrie was safe. I prayed for George too, unsure of whether he was at home when the storm hit. My prayers were turning to those in Iowa just as I crossed the border into dreamland.

That night the house creaked in the west wind. However, when I awoke in the morning, it was still and clear outside. As soon as I could, I got to the telephone and tried to call home, but the lines were down. I cooked breakfast, and the men went out to see about the horses and shovel out the doorways. When they came in, Gale said, "We have a little sleigh, Bessie. Once I get it rigged up, I can take you home."

As much as I enjoyed being with the Muirs and hated the tension at home, I had to admit to a bit of homesickness. How had my family fared? Did Carrie make it home okay? Therefore, we left the house about noon. The world had changed in one night from the golden browns of fall to sparkling white. The snow was perhaps a foot deep and not likely to last since it was not yet Thanksgiving, but it was pretty. I was tongue-tied as the horse trotted along.

"Caught you!" Gale said.

"What?"

"Caught you smiling about something." He was looking at me out the corner of his eyes as he had the day before. A wool hat completely covered his red hair.

"Oh, it's so beautiful out. I can't help but enjoy the scenery," I answered, but in the back of my mind something troubled me. "Gale, why did you stay in Minnesota so long, if I may ask?"

"It takes a lot to get two families packed up and moved here. Along with Janet and Albert, my brother, Will, is thinking about coming out too."

"Is that all?" It took all of my courage to ask, but I had nothing to lose and my curiosity got the best of me.

"Well, there is a certain girl there…"

"Yes?"

"Well, we're engaged to be married. But she can't leave her family just yet."

"I'm surprised you moved here without her."

"Yes, there are a lot of surprising things," he said. "Look at the creek. It's rising a surprising amount. You'd think it would be frozen after the storm."

Back at home, our whole family was out shoveling snow, although it looked to me like the boys were doing more snowball making than actual work. Carrie, Edwin, and Bill came running down the driveway when they saw the sleigh; their boots made the powdery snow fly. Suddenly I felt so strange, driving in with Gale as if he was my beau. Which of course he was not! He was an engaged man who happened to deliver me, the hired help, home.

"Bessie! Bessie! You are okay! We tried to call, but the telephone line is down," Carrie shouted soon enough. She was breathless, but that did not stop her from talking as she ran. "I almost got lost in the snow! If Billy had not known the way, I would be off somewhere on the prairie never to be found again. I could have died!"

"Whoa! Whoa!" Gale said to the horses, as Carrie skidded right up to the sleigh. The boys were right behind her. She opened her mouth to say more and then shut it as she spied Gale. Her eyes got big and round.

Turning to Gale, I said, "This is my sister, Carrie. And there are Bill and Edwin, my little brothers." I turned to Carrie and said, "This is Gale Muir. He just arrived from Jackson a few days ago and was kind enough to offer me a ride." I jumped down from the sleigh. "Gale, please come in for some hot cocoa."

He had removed his hat, and the sun glinted off his copper-colored hair. "Pleased to meet all of you, but I better get on home and help clean out the farmyard." He tipped his hat and clucked at the horses. Turning a wide circle in the yard, he made his way back to the road.

"Oh-oh, Bessie has a beau!" Bill chortled.

"You shush up. I work for his parents, that's all," I said. I picked up my satchel and headed toward the house. "Don't you have work to do?" I asked them, nodding to the heaps of snow in the yard.

Carrie followed me into the house. As we stamped snow off our shoes and shed our coats, she began to tell me her story. "I dismissed school when it started to snow. Then I banked the fire and straightened things up, saddled Billy up, and headed out. By that time, the wind was whipping the snow around. I passed a couple of farms and then headed toward the creek. You could hardly see. I got across the bridge okay, and then Billy and I had a fight. I wanted to go one way, and he wanted to go another. I whipped his behind with the reins, but he just kept going his own way. It seemed like a long time before he stopped, and when the wind let up, I could see we were between the barn and the house! How did he know where to go?" All of this spilled out, practically as one sentence.

"Oh, Carrie, I was worried about you and am so glad to see you here and safe! Maybe you should give up your teaching post. It could be a long, dangerous winter."

"Don't worry, Bessie. As long as I can ride Billy, I'll be safe," Carrie said. Then she motioned to me to follow her up to our room.

27

"Bessie, what's going on with Mother and Al?" Carrie asked several days later when we were in our room using the good south light to work on needle projects.

It was the day after Thanksgiving. The church had held a community Thanksgiving Dinner, and we'd spent days preparing food. We'd sung "My Country 'Tis of Thee," bowed our heads in thanksgiving, and then gorged ourselves on the bounty of our neighborhood harvest. Today we finally had some spare time to spend together.

"They're hardly speaking to each other," Carrie continued. "Things have sure changed. No more lovey-dovey business. It's more like an armed truce around here."

Apparently, Carrie did not know about the pie-pan argument. Although I had my own suspicions about Al pilfering the crop money to fund his gambling habit, I did not want to say anything yet.

"I don't know, Carrie. Maybe you should ask Mother what's going on."

"She'd just tell me to mind my own business. I personally think she has trouble getting along with men. First Father and now Al. She wants to be the boss. That is what I think. Al is a decent man. He's always in a good mood, and Mother can be cantankerous."

"Huh," I said. She really did not have a clue about what was going on.

"I am not impressed by people with smooth words, like Al Roots," I remarked. With that, I pushed my glasses up my nose and began threading a needle.

A few minutes later, Carrie brought up another sensitive topic. "Did you know I am crocheting these mittens to send to Joe for Christmas?" she asked. "Are you making him anything?"

I had all but forgotten about Joe. Because of my new job and the troubles at home, Joe had slipped into a spare room of my mind. Carrie still faithfully sent packages for his birthday and Christmas. A twinge of guilt twisted in my heart.

"I will bake some cookies and make fudge for your package," I volunteered.

"Don't you wonder how he is? Don't you wonder how Father is doing? I do. I want very badly to know they're okay."

"Why not write to the home and ask about Joe and write to Aunt Annie and ask what she knows about Father?" I suggested.

"Do you think Mother would be mad at me?

"Probably. However, it might give you peace of mind. It has been six years. Father may not even be around Fort Dodge any more. As for me, I cannot dwell on the past or I get all stirred up inside. You should not either. There are some things we can change and some we cannot. It is not our duty to take care of Joe and Father."

Carrie decided to write a letter to the Iowa Institute for Feeble-Minded Children, and I agreed to write to Aunt Annie.

> *Dear Aunt Annie,*
>
> *I trust you are all well. We have had our first winter storm. Carrie teaches in a country school four miles west of here and got caught in the storm. She is home safe because our horse Billy used his "horse sense" and found his way home.*
>
> *I work for a new family that moved here, the Muirs and their youngest son Gale. Several of their grown children are moving here also.*
>
> *Eddie often entertains us with the piano and his horn. Bill is growing so tall. We wrapped up the harvest. Today, after we cleared the snow out, Mother baked kolaches. Al went to town again.*

Is it possible that you know where Father is? Carrie stews about him. It would give her some peace to know what happened to him. You helped me find a way to forgive him. I hope you can help Carrie by sending some news.

Please greet everyone and give Babi a kiss for me.

Your niece,
Bessie

I was surprised to receive a letter from Aunt Annie the very next week.

Dear Bessie,

How wonderful to hear from you. I gave Babi your kiss at the first possible chance. She patted my hand and whispered your name. She is mostly bedridden now, but she loves to hear news about everyone.

The family is doing fine. Emma does most of the housekeeping for me. She is sweet on a local man, but we hope she will soon forget him. Elizabeth has finished her schooling and is living at home. She tires so easily that she cannot hire out to anyone. Little Rose is now twelve! She has turned into a young lady. The boys are all fine. They work for us or for the neighbors.

Thank you for the update. I am so grateful to hear Carrie made it through the storm. Your father is working for a farmer east of here. By chance, I saw him one day, walking along the tracks toward town. There is a rumor that he may end up in the Cherokee State Mental Hospital. I'm sorry to give you the news, but please know it may help if he goes there.

*How I wish you could join us for our
Thanksgiving feast this year!*

*Your aunt,
Annie Wesley Spirek*

Father was alive and working in Webster County but obviously was still having problems. As soon as possible, I showed the letter to Carrie.

"Why was he walking along the railroad tracks?" she asked right away. "Doesn't he even own a horse anymore? Oh, I wish I could do something for him! Do you think I could write him?"

The thought of bringing him back into our lives sent a finger of cold fear through me.

"Oh, Carrie, we don't know why he was walking there. Is it not enough to know he is alive and able to go for a walk? And that he lives in Webster County?"

"I don't know," she said, a perplexed look on her face.

"We have enough to deal with, so do not borrow trouble," I said, giving her my whole stock of sage advice. Then to distract her, I switched the subject. "Are you ever going to finish that rug you're braiding?"

"Oh, the rug!" Her face brightened. "Aren't the colors beautiful? Maybe I will finish it when I do not have all those classes to prepare for. I am lucky if I get to read the newspaper in the evening, and now I am working on Christmas projects too. It's going to take a month of Sundays to finish that rug!"

Carrie and I were so different. She loved getting out in the world, found interest in things faraway, and, I suspected, secretly believed in women's suffrage. I remained content to let others deal with the world. I did not plan to venture beyond my own little corner.

I loved Carrie a lot and sometimes wondered what my life might have been like had she died of the fever in 1899. One of my favorite times of the day was when I brushed her hair at night, although I would not let her do mine because she yanked the brush through it something terrible. We would yak about hair and clothing styles and all but memorized the Sears and Roebuck catalogues when they came out. We gossiped about which girls secretly wore rouge or lipstick or who had a beau.

We also had an invisible bond because of what we had endured together, but we never talked about the past outside the walls of our room.

The letter from Aunt Annie seemed to comfort Carrie. We shipped a package to Joe that held mittens, a cap, cookies, and fudge. We also tucked in some hard Christmas candy. A few weeks later, the Home wrote to Carrie thanking her for the package and saying Joe was fine.

28

Through that winter of 1906–1907, I divided my time between home and the Muir household. Gale drove me when he was at LaMoure, although he did make a trip back to Jackson. We did not talk about personal things much. I assumed by the letters Gale sent and received that his romance was going well, although apparently no wedding date was set.

I liked to join other young people in the neighborhood, even if we just gathered around a piano somewhere to sing. Eddie had the sheet music for a new song sweeping the country called "The Grand Old Flag." I had my favorites too, like "Bill Bailey Won't You Please Come Home" and "In the Good Old Summer Time."

Despite money being tight, Mother bought a New Home sewing machine for fifteen dollars that fall. I learned to operate it as soon as possible. What a treat to stitch up a new dress on that machine, although I heard the newer Singers were far superior.

Now that I was a working girl, I purchased new fabric with my own money. I had two heavy cotton work dresses with skirts full enough so I could move around in them, but not so full as to get in the way. Mother helped me make a good blue wool suit for dress-up occasions and a riding outfit. For every day, I generally wore shirt-waists and skirts. Although great big hats were the fashion, I favored perky little ones that better suited my small frame. I did not care a whit for jewelry and silk dresses, which was good as there was no money for such things.

The LaMoure area was progressing. In town, a new brick schoolhouse had opened, and new businesses seemed to spring up every week. You could even buy an automobile in LaMoure. I could hardly believe my eyes when I first saw one huffing and popping along the street, kicking up more dust than a team of horses.

Quite a few members of the Muir family arrived during this land boom. As I mentioned before, John and Lena Muir and family were the first Muirs to arrive. I wondered how many kitchen table conversations took place at Jackson, as John convinced the others to pull up roots and settle in North Dakota.

Gale's sister, Kate, and her husband, Arthur Raub, had arrived in LaMoure late in the summer of 1906. He worked in town, and they had two little ones. Melville was two, and Iva was born just after they arrived in North Dakota.

Another of Gale's sisters, Janet, and her husband, Albert Hunt, had the most land, 480 acres. They were older when they married and had no children. A former schoolteacher, Janet helped her mother on the days I was not there. In her wedding picture, Janet wore a beautiful suit that she made herself.

Another brother, Will, purchased land in LaMoure County, but he and his family remained in Jackson. Some cousins of the Muirs lived in the vicinity also.

I sometimes imagined what it would be like to have my Spirek relatives move to North Dakota. Land's sake, how wonderful to plan Thanksgiving, Christmas, and Easter with them again or to meet them at Grand Rapids Park on Independence Day. However, I would soon grab my thoughts and push them into the present. One cannot step into the future with one foot in the past. Who knew what the future might hold? After all, I had never dreamed I would live anywhere but Webster County, but here I was.

It was funny about Janet Hunt and me though. I could not seem to win her approval. She sometimes redid things on the weekend that I had already worked on, like shining the windows or putting a new coat of polish on the cook stove. I always did my best, so I was not sure why she did it again.

Then there was an issue with Gale. When Janet found us talking, she always gave off an air of disapproval. Land's sake! What kind of person did she think I was? Some kind of trollop? I knew Gale's heart belonged to another, but here I was living in the same house for part of the week. Not visiting with him would have been downright rude. Janet would have been the first to point that out.

I suppose I could have refused to let him drive me back and forth, but it was a great help to have him do so. Of course, Al Roots or George could have given me a ride, but Al liked to sleep late in the mornings, and George often hired out for room and board. I could have ridden over myself too, but Gale always seemed to be there with his buggy.

Janet made it clear she thought very highly of Gale's fiancée. I guessed that was because her father was the Presbyterian minister in Jackson. Clergy rated high with Janet.

I did not hear the same kind of excitement from Robert and Mary Muir. They were cordial in what they said about this woman in Minnesota. However, Robert Muir sometimes teased Gale about his coming difficulties with marrying an only child who had been spoiled by her parents. I do not think I was meant to hear that. I also wondered how this "bride" felt about moving to North Dakota and sharing a house with her in-laws, for surely that was how it was going to work. However, it was not my problem.

True, Gale made my heart flutter. Not only was he good-looking but he also had a wonderful dry wit. He was a hard worker and an expert hunter. I liked the way he treated his mother. He was even kind to the farm animals and the hired help.

But that was neither here nor there. He planned to marry another woman. My plan was to remain single. No marriage for me, after watching my mother's marriages. I was not going to bother tying the knot with someone who turned out to be a drinker like Father, or a crook, which is what I thought of Al Roots. No, I was staying single. So let Janet Hunt think what she wanted.

But, quite honestly—outside of our neighbors in Iowa who gossiped about our family, I got along with everyone, so Janet's attitude really bothered me. Finally, I confided in Carrie, who jumped to my defense. "Humph! I will tell her she is not so high and mighty! And I'll tell her our uncles own half of Webster County!"

"Land's sake, don't do that!" I was brushing Carrie's hair by lamplight and she would not hold still, so the brush had to follow the movement of her head. "I'd rather give a soft answer to win her over."

The next week, I had other thoughts when Janet came right out and said she did not think women should remarry when their husbands died, or worse, if women divorced their husbands. She was not talking directly to me, but I felt the stab of her words. Did she somehow know Mother was divorced? My face reddened.

This time when I told Carrie about it, I sputtered my frustration and anger.

"That's the spirit, Bessie. Don't let her get away with saying things. Let her have it!"

Should I? It seemed like someone should put Janet in her place, but was that my job? I had been walking in a quiet world of forgiveness for some time now, and it felt good to be free of the savage emotions that had ruled my heart. Forgiving the past was one thing, but perhaps I should see if I could forgive Janet now and again if she said or did more insulting things.

A smile spread across my face. "Carrie, I'm going to try something else—being so sweet to her that she's embarrassed for the things she says."

I did that through the winter of 1906–1907. Whenever I saw Janet, I complimented her. In fact, I tried to think of things beforehand that I could say. "Your hair is lovely." Or "That dress is so becoming." "That is the best squash dish I've ever had!" On and on. At first, she looked at me very closely, as though trying to discover whether I really meant what I said. I would just stare back at her and smile, until she realized she needed to thank me for the compliment. However, the icicles never thawed off her that year.

Our church services were still at the school. When the road was not icy or muddy, we sometimes walked there. Mother seemed most at peace on Sundays, as though the services quieted her spirit. Back at home, she took to playing Bohemian dirges on the piano again, as she had done when things were going badly with Father. Carrie and

I finally ordered some sheet music for her from the Sears & Roebuck catalogue, mostly hymns to sooth her brooding soul.

One day in the spring of 1907, while cleaning house, I found a letter Mother had tucked under the ink blotter on the desk. She had started to write her brother, Anton. .No one else was around, so I sat at the desk and read it quickly.

> *Dear Anton,*
>
> *I trust you and yours are doing well. Please greet everyone for me, since I am not much at letter writing. My hip is bothering me where I took that fall. Otherwise, we are all fine.*
>
> *I am writing for some brotherly advice. I do not know what to do anymore. I think Al lies about the money he gets for the crops, but I cannot prove it. I hardly have enough money to make the farm payments and buy seed for next year's crop. Thank goodness George, Bessie, and Carrie all have jobs and help out. That fox loses money playing cards, I think. He says I am crazy for not trusting him. I am plum tired of it all. You can guess that, or I would not be writing to you.*

She had not finished writing the letter. I slid it back under the blotter. When had she written this? Poor Mother, she must be beside herself, I thought. Seeing the letter put some starch in my back. Before I had suspicions about Al Roots, but I could not really say they were based on fact. Now I knew my instincts were right. I decided to watch him like a dog guarding a farmyard.

29

April 1907

''Mirror, mirror on the wall, Bessie's fairest of them all!''

"Mirror, mirror on the wall, please tell Carrie she's got it all!"

We stood side by side, our heads leaning together, staring in the bureau mirror. We were in our pantaloons and camisoles, fresh out of the galvanized tub we had dragged up to our room. We had worked out a system for bathing in privacy since our house did not have a bathroom. We heated water on the kitchen range and lugged it up the stairs. After our baths, we pitched the water out the window to the ground below, so we did not have to lug it back down. We doubted Mother would mind, although we did not tell her about our ingenuity.

We had taken turns in the tub and now stood wrapped in robes, studying ourselves in the mirror. Carrie was half a head taller than me. We both had dark hair, darker now because it was still wet. We had the same jawline, though Carrie's features were heavier than mine were. She had grown up to be full-bodied like our mother and grandmother. I was as scrawny as a stray cat and plain flat in the chest area, which bothered me more than wearing glasses. At least my spectacles helped me see, but what was the point of being flat-chested?

It was a warm spring Saturday night, and we were preparing for the pot blessing after church the next day. Cottonwood Church loved a good social. We had been talking about what to wear and how to do our hair all afternoon as we cooked and baked for the next day.

Still looking in the mirror, I said, "Carrie, you have what every girl wants, and I don't have one."

A questioning frown crossed her face.

"A bosom!" I explained.

"Oh pshaw, who cares about that? Bessie, you are so little and cute, and you have such a winning smile. All the boys are sweet on you. Especially Gale Muir." She arched a dark brow at me.

I felt my face color. Why must I always defend myself? I did not say or do a thing to suggest a romance with Gale, but Carrie and my brothers still gave me a bad time about him.

"Not only that, I heard his engagement isn't going so well," she added.

"Who said that?"

"A friend. She told me all about how that got started and what a spoiled preacher's daughter she is. Seems her folks cannot find anyone else to marry her. Gale got pulled into it because he did not know how to say no," Carrie said with a sniff. She loved a good scandal, as long as it was not in our family.

I wondered where the friend got her information. Certainly it was not from Gale's sister, Janet.

"So that doesn't mean the engagement isn't going well. But it's true, he's sometimes too nice for his own good," I said. "But he seems very devoted to her. He writes letters."

"Devoted to *her*? If he were devoted to her, he would be driving her around Jackson. He picks you up for work and makes sure you are safe even in the nastiest weather. He grins all the time when you are around. He hasn't been back to Jackson all winter."

"Not so," I said. "He was there for Christmas. He is leaving for Jackson again as soon as the crop is in. He won't be back until haying begins."

Carrie snorted. "Oh, so you know his plans?"

"Why shouldn't I? I work over there. The family talks. Gale tells me what he's doing."

"Well, if you ask me, there's a girl in Jackson who's going to have a broken heart before long."

I backed away from the mirror. We would have to go down to the kitchen to heat the curling iron on the stove and finish our hair once we threw out the bathwater. I tried to picture Gale breaking his engagement. The thought made me smile. From what I knew of him, there was no way he could do it.

"Well, we'll see. 'Tis been a long engagement. Maybe he'll come back a married man," I mused.

The thought darkened my heart like a big cloud moving over the sun. In the last seven or eight months, Gale and I had never held hands or kissed, but I'd certainly thought a lot about it, especially at night when I lay awake as he slept down the hall. One thing I knew for certain: if he married someone else, I would lose a good friend.

I wondered how I could stand to be around the happy new couple. Or Janet. She would gloat that her brother had married a preacher's daughter and not some hired girl with a murky past. Not that Janet knew about us being Catholic, that Mother was divorced, or we had a brother in an institution. But somehow, her eyes always accused me of being less than I should be.

Could I bear to live here with the newlyweds right down the road? Certainly, I would not hire out to the Muirs anymore.

My thoughts took me down another path. What would Mother say if I went back to Iowa and worked for one of my uncles? They always needed an extra pair of hands. I knew now that Mother was seeking advice from her brother Anton. Maybe Mother wanted to move back to Iowa. Then I would be right back in the boiling pot, dealing with Father and the past we put behind us. I sighed, resigned to live out a miserable life in Cottonwood Township if Gale came back from Jackson a married man.

The pot blessing took place on a clear, sunny day. The scent of apple and plum blossoms wafted through the air, although they had not yet bloomed. Once again, we had a wonderful time with our friends and neighbors in Cottonwood Township, confirming that moving here indeed was a good choice.

Time seemed to speed by. We had a pretty spring that year, and the crops promised to be the best ever. It seemed to rain at the right time, and the sun shone every day. Farmers talked of a bumper crop and hoped the markets would stabilize.

Gale did go back to Minnesota, saying he would not be gone long because of the work waiting here. Of course, I knew it would not take any time at all for a preacher to marry off his daughter in their front room. Not any time at all.

30

June 1907

That summer, Mother often sent me to town on my days off. I would hitch Bump to the buggy, and off we would go. I always had errands to run, but my understood purpose was to get the mail. I would thumb through the mail looking for a letter from Uncle Anton. So far, he had not written.

Then one day, I came home from work just as Al Roots came from town. He dropped the mail on the dining room table. I stopped right away to see what had come in.

A letter from Uncle Anton lay at the top of the pile, the envelope open. When Mother came in wiping her hands on her apron to sift through the mail, Al just stood there and stared at the letter and then at her. It was obviously a private moment, but I did not budge from the room.

"What? Al, are you opening my mail now?" Mother said.

"I thought we was married," he answered. "Doesn't that mean your mail is my mail?"

"Why would you care what Anton writes? You hardly know him or his family."

"I know you've been writing to your brother to whine about me. That much I know." Al took a step toward Mother, and I jerked forward, ready to defend her.

Then Al burst out laughing. "Hahaha! Oh, Mary. You are such a silly goose. Asking Anton for advice."

Then he turned toward me. "You are going to have to watch your mother, Bessie. I think she is getting funny in the head. Make sure she doesn't wander off and get lost or something."

Turning back to Mother, he said, "Don't even think about following through on Anton's advice, Mary, because I have friends in town," he threatened before wandering outside, still laughing.

Mother's face was beet red. Her mouth worked like Carrie's did when she got good and upset. She looked shocked and began to shake all over. With quivering fingers, she picked up the letter. I put on my spectacles and looked over her shoulder. In part, the letter read:

> *Thank you for remembering what good advice I give. As for the pickle you are in, I would visit with the elevator manager this fall and arrange to have all payments made directly to the bank. That way, whoever takes the harvest in will get a receipt, but not the payment. Therefore, if Al is lining his pockets, you can nip off his little scam.*

There could not have been a worse end for Anton's letter than to fall into Al's hands. Mother picked up the poker from beside the stove in the living room and swung it around, then seemed to realize she looked more than a little crazy. She put the poker down and sat in a chair, her head down, her fists flexing.

"What am I going to do, Bessie?" Mother's voice was soft, and she seemed beaten down like when her marriage to Father was falling apart.

I sat on the sofa next to her and patted her hand, rubbing it between my own. Her hands were rough with work, and her knuckles thickened with arthritis. "We'll think of something," I comforted, though no ideas came to my head. "We will. Maybe you can still talk to the grain buyer."

Mother shook her head. Men did not respect a woman over her husband, and the men in town knew Al Roots better than they knew her. Al would surely lead them to think she was getting strange in the head.

George often worked for other farmers now that our crop was in. When he came home that weekend, I asked him to go for a walk with me. We strolled off to the west, along Cottonwood Creek. Prairie flowers grew so thick in the pasture there that I lost track of all the different varieties, from wild roses and daisies to Canadian thistle. We finally found a lovely meadow where we sat near the creek that bubbled by.

When I told George all I knew about Al Roots, he seemed surprised. While I saw a lot of the dark side of Al, he had only seen the nice fellow who treated him well. We talked a long time and, truthfully, I was not sure he really believed me. However, he promised to keep an eye open for underhanded doings. I hoped he would be around to take the crops to market during harvest, but it was not likely, since he often hired out to others.

31

Over the next several weeks, my heart remained heavy and distracted by Mother's ordeal. I could feel myself sinking into a dark state again.

I rode to work bareback after Gale went to Minnesota, but the day after he got home, he was at our door to pick me up. The morning was still but for the call of morning birds. The orange and purple sunrise was well worth rising early. We rode in silence for a while.

Finally, Gale said, "Well, I expected a better welcome than this."

"Oh," I said. "Welcome back. Did you have a good trip?"

"Yes."

"Did you…Did you come back alone?" I asked.

"Yes. Who did you think would come with me? *Another* relative?"

"In a manner of speaking," I said, not wanting to mention the fiancée. We rode the rest of the way in silence. Neighbors came to help cut hay, so there were more men to cook for and they were hungry. I made a beef roast and potatoes for our big meal at noon, with rhubarb pie for dessert. For dinner, we had chicken and dumplings, topped off with spice cake. In between, I took sandwiches, cookies, and lemonade to the field for lunch.

Because the days were long and my family's haying would not begin for a few days, I stayed overnight. It was well into the evening when I finally put the beans to soaking. In the morning, I would cook ham and beans for the noon meal. It was twilight, about 10:00 p.m., by the time I took my apron off and walked outside. Oh, it was so beautiful, and much cooler than in the kitchen. I strolled along the driveway and headed across the road to Cottonwood Creek to soak my feet in the cool water.

"Bessie, wait up!" Gale waved his hat and hurried toward me. I wondered if it was proper for us to be walking alone so close to dark. With my luck, Janet and Albert would come driving up and think we were doing something scandalous. *But,* I thought, *Janet should be home in bed by this hour.*

We walked along in silence for a while before Gale asked why I was so quiet. Suddenly a tear sprang from my eye and rolled down my cheek. How could I ever tell this nice man about our family's dilemma? I took a deep breath and kept walking.

"If you haven't noticed, I'm a pretty good listener," he offered. "And I promise not to tell Janet anything you say."

That brought a smile to my face. Gale must have seen the tension between his sister and me. "Well, 'tis family business. I don't think Mother or George would like me talking about it."

"Must be about Al Roots then."

"How did you know?" I asked before I could stop myself.

"Just a good guess. He likes to play cards in town, and he has lost a bunch of money. I would bet my best hat your mother doesn't know about that."

We had arrived at the creek and found a place to sit down. We took off our shoes and dangled our feet in the water. It felt so soft and cool. Once again, sitting by the creek, I told the story of the crop money, as I had told it to George. I even told Gale about the letters between Mother and Uncle Anton and how I did not think even George believed me.

"I believe you," Gale said simply. "And you can call me any time you might need help."

"I don't think your fiancée would appreciate you making promises like that."

"Well, I thought about that on the train ride back to North Dakota," said Gale. "That woman, she's a challenge. Truthfully, I expected to get married in Jackson, but we got into a tiff. She will not come out here to live. She acted as if it was all settled for me to move back there."

Gale gave a bewildered chuckle before continuing. "Then she and her mama began talking about the wedding. Before I could say 'whoa there,' it had become a big dumb wedding. It would take a year to plan it. Before I left, she said her mama would fix up a room for us in the parsonage so we could live with them."

Gale sat facing the water as his indignation spilled out. It somehow tickled my funny bone, but I dared not laugh. "Oh," I said, not trusting myself to say more. I concentrated on drawing my feet out of the water to dry.

"So you see," Gale continued, "on the way back from Minnesota, I decided to send her a letter. I sat in the lobby of the Windsor Hotel in LaMoure when I got off the train and I wrote it. Took it to the post office before I came home."

"Ohhh," I said.

"I told her my life was out here. I was sorry she did not want to move to North Dakota with me. I said she was a fine woman. Most of that's the truth. Well, some of it is the truth. Then I asked her to break the engagement."

"What's true and what isn't?" I asked, hardly daring to breathe.

"Well, my life is here now. That is the truth. However, I was not sorry she did not want to move out here. When I was in Jackson, I was hoping she would let me loose. And I'm still afraid she won't let me out of the engagement."

"Why, Gale!" I had to laugh at this turn of events. Here I thought he would come back married and instead he was almost a free man.

"So you see, Bessie, I really meant it when I said you can count on me."

I could not help it then. I threw my arms around him and hugged him tight there with the sky filling up with stars and the night birds calling. Gale bent down, his lips touching mine. I felt like lightning zinged me. It was my first kiss, and it was a good one. Just then, a noisy mosquito came by my neck, and I slapped at it. Gale slapped at another. Then I noticed a noise up on the road. A wagon was rolling by in the darkness, the clip-clop of horse hooves competing with the squeak and whine of the wheels.

"We better go!" I said, slipping on my stockings and shoes, afraid of my feelings and thankful for the interruptions.

"Bessie, wait, I have a question to ask you." Gale was on his knees, his boots in his hand. I had already stood up. He grabbed my hand and asked, "Bessie, once I've heard from her, can I court you? I, well, I really like you a lot."

"Court me?" Why land's sake. That was the last thing I expected to hear that night. "Yes, you may court me!" I said.

We walked back through the pasture hand in hand, the scent of flowers filling the air. Back in the house, we took off our shoes, trying to be quiet, but an occasional giggle slipped out. We tiptoed up the dark stairs, parting ways at the door to my room. I swear I saw Mr. Muir peeking through a crack in their bedroom door, but it was so dark I could not tell for sure.

The next evening when Gale took me home, Carrie was bent over the flowerbed in front of the house pulling weeds. She sat up and looked at us. Gale and I both blushed. I said a quick good-bye and jumped down from the buggy seat, my satchel in hand.

As soon as Gale was out of hearing range, Carrie said, "So is Gale married? He does not look very married."

"No, he is not married," I said. It would not be proper to tell her he was not going to marry his Minnesota fiancée, since the lady did not know yet herself. I quickly skirted past her to the door.

"Well, I bet he's going to marry you!" Carrie called after me.

Then strangely, the rest of the summer I hardly saw Gale. It was not proper for us to court before his fiancée broke the engagement, and Gale faithfully kept up appearances of devotion to her. I took to sleeping at home rather than staying overnight at the Muir's, and I rode my horse to work. We both attended social events, but never together. In any case, Carrie was seventeen and always went with me, an eager chaperone.

"Why doesn't he act like your beau?" Carrie accused one day in August. It was Sunday, and we had wandered down to the creek in the middle of the afternoon. The hot wind was preparing the fields for harvest in a few days. Carrie and I sat on the creek bank, our feet roaming the cool, muddy creek bottom. The water level had dropped a lot in the last month.

"He's not my beau."

"Well, what happened to the preacher's daughter in Minnesota? Why doesn't he marry her?" Carrie pried.

"Carrie, are you feeling better about, you know, about Joe and Father these days?" I asked to change the subject. Distracted, she immediately began to talk about them, Gale forgotten.

I barely listened, my mind wandering. I did not know what to think about Gale. He had been friendly but distant all summer. Surely, the woman in Minnesota had given him an answer by now. The longer and hotter the summer got, the sillier I got. I forgot my decision to never marry. Now, if he asked me, I wanted to say yes. I hardly thought of anything but the kind, handsome redhead.

32

September 1907

I was in the garden behind the house the day Bill ran out and said I had a phone call. It was September, and we had canned, dried, or stored most of our produce. However, I still found nice tomatoes to slice for dinner every day. I held a load of tomatoes in my apron and ran to the house. It was not very often I got a phone call.

"Bessie?" the voice in the receiver sounded like Gale. Was it? He had never called me before, so I was not sure.

"Yes, this is Bessie."

"A flock of geese landed on the Jim due east of your place, and I was wondering if you would go hunting with me this afternoon? I'll help you saddle up that Morgan, and we can cut across country."

I was quiet for a moment. Was this a practical joke? I wheeled around looking for Bill, sure he was trying to trick me, but he was nowhere to be seen. The next second, I decided it really was Gale on the phone, and he was serious.

"You want to go hunting?" I asked incredulously.

"Will you go with me, Bessie? I have something to discuss with you."

"I'm not much of a hunter," I volunteered. "But I'll go with you. How about if I pack a picnic lunch instead of a gun?" I thought about my little pistol tucked away in a drawer. What would Gale think if he knew I owned a gun and why?

"That sounds like a deal," he said, bringing me back to the present. "Do you have any of those sour cream sugar cookies?"

"I'll have some when you get here," I answered smartly. After hanging up the receiver, I stood for a minute staring at the phone in shock. After waiting to hear from Gale for months, it finally had happened. What would he have to say?

After the noon meal, I baked sugar cookies. While they were in the oven, I sliced up the leftover roast beef and made some hearty sandwiches slathered with horseradish, which I knew Gale liked. For drinks, I mixed up a Mason jar of Watkin's nectar. Then I borrowed saddlebags from George and filled them with the food, a small square tablecloth, our prettiest glasses, and plates and napkins.

Gale arrived promptly at four o'clock. I was still upstairs in my room. I would like to say I was getting ready to go, but the truth was I had been loitering behind the curtain, watching for him, butterflies in my stomach.

Mother answered the door when he knocked, and I strained to hear the conversation. They exchanged a few polite words about the weather and the harvest before Gale came right out and said, "Mrs. Roots, do you mind if I begin to court Bessie?"

I covered my mouth in delight and strangled my handkerchief with nervousness while listening for Mother's answer.

The pause seemed to go on forever before Mother spoke. "That would be fine, Gale, as long as your intentions are honorable. If you take her anywhere in the evening, of course I will expect you to take others with you. During the day, it's fine if you go for a ride or something."

I let out my breath, not realizing I had been holding it. Mother and I had never once talked about Gale or about any boy or man for that matter. I had no idea what she would say, but she was downright cordial. I took off for the stairs, eager to leave with Gale.

"You looked just grand riding off together," Carrie later said. She had cut through the trees and watched us go down the section line. "There you were, man and woman, riding those two magnificent horses," she said dramatically. "You sat so straight in the saddle, your dress flowing over Bump's rump just like you were a Spanish donna. The chokecherry leaves were purple and the apricot leaves gold. Oh my, you made quite a picture. I thought right then and there, 'I have lost a sister, but I will gain a brother-in-law.' It brought tears to my eyes."

Of course, I knew none of what she was thinking at the time. I will not forget the black riding suit I made when Mother gave me my horse and buggy. There had not been much chance to wear it, but on this fall day, it seemed perfect. I also wore a little black fedora with a long blue scarf wound around it. Gale had on a white shirt and dark brown leather vest, the kind that looks soft and worn and comfortable. He also had on his riding fedora and had two guns secured on his saddle. He was quite handsome that day, for sure. His hunting dog, Homer, trotted along beside us.

We were hardly out of earshot when Gale said he had received his ring back.

"Is your fiancée mad at you?"

"I don't know. She did not write a word. However, my sister Minnie sent a letter and said she had taken up with a man from a nearby town. I guess she didn't want to let me go until she had another fellow to stand in as the groom in her big wedding."

We rode a little further, and then Gale began laughing. "Boy, you should have seen Janet sputter when she heard the news."

"Hmmm," I said, a little smile playing at my lips. "What about the rest of your family?"

"No one seemed surprised or upset," Gale said a little quizzically. "But right away, my mother asked if I'd seen you lately. I figured that was Morse code for she hoped I'd see you soon."

We traveled past a couple fields and wound our way south, about a half-mile from Janet and Albert's farm. Then we made our way down toward the river. We did not talk, just made sure we got safely down into the valley. When we came to a grassy pasture on the river, Gale stopped. Homer kept sniffing the air and bounding off in his own direction.

"This would be a good place to watch for the geese," Gale said. He got off his horse and whistled for the dog. I got down and went to stand at the river. We had been in Dakota over three years by then. I had spent countless hours by Cottonwood Creek, but not much time by the James River. Where the creek was small and comforting, the river seemed wide and mysterious.

"Sit here, Bessie," Gale said, flopping down on the grass and patting a spot next to him. He took off his hat and laid it down. Once I sat and had my skirts adjusted, he reached in his pocket and gave me a packet of pins.

"What is this for?"

Gale cleared his throat. "I was trying to think of a gift for you to show how much I care." He began blushing, and his face turned almost the same color as his hair. "Now it seems more foolish than anything I've done. I should have brought you flowers or perfume."

I just looked at him and at the pins. This seemed odder than his asking me to go hunting right out of the clear blue sky when he had hardly talked to me all summer.

Gale cleared his throat again and began to sing. "I give to you a packet of pins, for that's the way true love begins, if you will marry me, me, me, if you will marry me."

I smiled and then laughed, but he did not laugh with me. "I guess giving you the pins is the silliest thing I ever did. Almost as silly as thinking maybe you'd consider marrying me."

I quickly sucked in my breath. "Land's sake, are you asking me to marry you? But this is only our first proper date!"

Gale seemed to color even deeper. "I've liked you since we first met, but I was tangled up with someone else, as you know." He took my hand and looked into my eyes. "I knew almost right away that I wanted to marry you. I've never felt that way about anyone else."

"Oh, Gale!"

"I am sorry if I seemed neglectful, but I couldn't trust myself to be around you this summer. I could not get our first kiss out of my mind. If you will have me, I do not want a long courtship. I love you, and I want to get married."

I looked down at his hand clenching mine. His hands were freckled, with golden hair on the top side, but the bottom was work-calloused. Sweat had broken out on his forehead.

"This must be the most romantic proposal any girl has ever had," I said. "I don't have to think about my answer too long. I would love to marry you!"

Gale pulled me to my feet then picked me up like a feather and whirled me around until we were both giddy with laughter. Then he stopped and kissed me long and hard. I thought my heart would melt.

It is good that Homer began barking up a storm about that time because we finally had to look up. When we did, a flock of geese was honking and flapping down from the sky toward the river. Gale let me go like a spring action toy and went for his gun. "Boy, first the prettiest girl in the county says yes to me and then a flock of geese goes right overhead!" he exclaimed.

I waved him off and watched as he and Homer disappeared over a rise. The gun went off a couple of times, causing the geese to honk frantically. The sound of hundreds of flapping wings filled the air as they looked for a safer place to settle for the night. A few minutes later, Gale and Homer appeared with two good-sized geese.

After admiring the feathery game, I laid out the tablecloth and lunch. I was anxious to please Gale and show him I had made a nice meal just for him. After eating our sandwiches and cookies, we talked until the sun disappeared and the evening got too chilly to sit any longer.

We decided to keep our intentions a secret for a couple of weeks, unsure of how our families might feel about the sudden plans. Of course, they did not seem sudden to us. It was more like our plans were just catching up with our feelings.

That evening, Carrie pumped me for details until I finally threw the bed pillows at her. "Go downstairs and work on your rug," I demanded, and she finally stomped off.

Once I was alone in the room, I knelt in front of the bureau and opened the bottom drawer. It had filled up with items for my hope chest—pillowcases, dishtowels, and doilies. At the bottom, under everything else was my little wicker sewing basket. I took it out and held it carefully, remembering how Aunt Annie and Babi had encouraged my sewing. Now I longed to talk with them. I hadn't told Mother or Carrie I was getting married, but I knew for sure if Aunt Annie was here, I'd let her in on the secret.

I opened the basket's lid and lifted out the thimbles and other notions. The veil Father had given me was tucked safely in the bottom. I lifted it out and put it on my head. It carried me back through the years to a time when Father lived with us, a time when our family had hope of staying together. The basket held only happy memories, and now I put the paper of pins in it.

As I put the basket back in the drawer, my hand hit the pistol I kept hidden there. How surprising to realize all of my anger toward Father had washed away. I remembered the bad things, but they did not hurt or make me angry any more. The basket and gun seemed to sum up my life to that point.

I knelt by the window and watched the stars twinkling so far away. I knew those same stars shone on Iowa. Dreamily, I wondered if Father could possibly be looking at those same stars or if he could sense the message my heart longed to send to him. "Oh Father," I whispered, "Please know that my life has turned out fine. I'm all grown up and getting married!"

My, how life had changed. That evening, I savored the wonder of my new love.

The rosy glow of our secret engagement lasted about twenty-four hours.

33

October 1907

Gale picked me up for work the next morning, and we stopped on the bridge and talked in excited whispers about the day before. I do not know why we whispered because there was not anyone within half a mile of us.

If I seemed unusually happy while working around the Muir place, no one said anything about it, although I blushed when Gale walked into the house for dinner and Mary Muir noticed. It seemed like she was trying to hide a smile.

When Janet came by, I could see she'd had a change of heart. Later, she took me aside and, squeezing my hand, thanked me for taking good care of her parents. Then she apologized for, perhaps, misjudging me.

Well, land's sake, I told her there was no need. I almost blurted out that soon we would be sisters-in-law and I hoped we would be friends too but somehow managed to keep my tongue. It was not until I was home again for the night that second thoughts began to crowd in. While the packet of pins seemed romantic and sweet to me, when I thought of telling Mother about it, the light of realism shone on it.

I could just hear Mother say if Gale could only afford to give me a bunch of stickpins for an engagement present, what kind of life would he provide? I was glad we had decided to keep our engagement secret for a while, because I absolutely could not have told Mother. I just knew she would pop my happy bubble.

I had overheard her say she married Father for love and that she would have done it again, despite all their problems and bad ending. She must have been in love with Al Roots too when they tied the knot. But her practical side certainly would not find anything romantic in a paper of pins.

I did not know how Carrie might react. She liked Gale a lot, especially after he brought her a stack of *Life* and *Saturday Evening Post* magazines when he came back from Jackson. However, Carrie also had a business head. She would wonder if Gale could provide for a wife and family.

Carrie evaluated every young man with a cold eye. Was he smart? Did he own a farm or a business? Did he keep up with politics? Oh, her list was very different from mine. I could not share my secret with her either because truthfully now I had doubts.

I hated that because I was in love with him. Not only did we get along great but I could also see his solid family background and knew we shared so many values. That seemed like enough. But was it?

I would have to think on this a while longer. After all, I had decided to never marry. It was only when Gale was around that I could not think straight. Now alone in my room, doubts started creeping in like mice through a hole in the wall. I remembered how he had given the girl in Minnesota a *ring*, while I received a *paper of pins*. In addition, despite his explanation, I puzzled over the fact that he had ignored me all summer.

Two days later, Gale invited me to take a buggy ride with him to the Dairy Bar in LaMoure. He could not believe I had never had an ice cream soda, so he planned to buy me my first. We bundled up pretty good, but truthfully, the cold air did not even register with me.

We had a wonderful time. The soda was delicious. People kept stopping by our booth to visit, and soon a couple of hours had flown by. It was starting to get dark and time to go home since we did not have a chaperone along. We left the Dairy Bar and got back in the buggy. Gale threw a wool blanket over our laps, and away we went. As soon as we crossed the river outside of town, he pulled into the little park beside the road. Usually there were fishermen standing along the bank, but today the place was deserted.

"I have a little something for you," Gale said as he wrapped the reins around the brake handle. He reached in his coat pocket and pulled out a tiny box. "I wish it was a great big diamond." With that, he handed me the box. I pulled off my gloves and opened it. A gold ring with a row of five pearls gleamed at me.

I was silent a minute, reeling with shame, remembering my greedy thoughts of wanting a ring like the girl in Minnesota. I was ashamed I had ever doubted this man. "It is beautiful!" I said, tracing the smooth tops of the pearls and fingering the shiny gold circle. "I have never had a gold ring before."

"My family isn't much for jewelry or flashy clothes," he explained. "The old Scottish ways, you know. However, I wanted to give you more than a paper of pins. I want people to know we are pledged to each other. I want to give you something pretty that you can keep forever and pass on to our children and grandchildren."

I slipped the ring on the fourth finger of my left hand, and Gale checked it out. "It's too big. The jeweler will have to resize it for you."

We sat and talked as the dusk crept in, staying until the horse began nickering, impatient for his evening oats. We decided to take the ring to be sized the next day. As soon as it was ready, we would announce our engagement.

I could not have guessed what a long delay loomed ahead of us.

34

The next morning before dawn, while Carrie and I were snug in our bed, an argument broke out in the kitchen below us. I slowly came awake. Mother and Al Roots were bickering. He wanted to take a load of grain to town, but Mother opposed him. I was not as surprised they were arguing as I was that Al was up so early.

Normally, he stayed in bed until Mother got the boys up to do chores and things were underway in the kitchen. Then he'd come downstairs, wearing pants with suspenders over his long underwear, to drink a cup of coffee at the dining room table and read the latest newspaper. He said he needed more rest and could not stand the racket of all us kids getting ready to go to work and school.

But this morning, he apparently considered selling the grain important enough to get him out of bed early. Eventually, the door slammed shut, and the kitchen became silent. I imagined Mother sitting alone in the dark, weighing the matter.

I rolled out of bed, grabbed my robe, and rushed down the stairs. The glow of the lamp in the kitchen shed light into the dining room, where Mother sat at the table. Her hair was messy, as though she had not bothered with it at all. She sat with her hand on her chin, her stout body sprawled on the chair. I remembered what Al Roots said about her getting funny in the head. In the predawn light, she looked like a wild woman.

As I had done once before when Father had battered her, I went to her and held her close. This time, there were no physical bruises, no flood of tears, only a sigh of resignation.

"He wanted to sell the grain," she explained.

"Did you do what Uncle Anton said?" I asked. "Did you talk to the elevator man? Did you tell him to just give Al a receipt for the grain?"

Outside, the sound of horse hooves beat by the house. That, too, reminded me of Father and the time he left during the night, changing our lives forever. I rushed to the window and saw Al turn south. Lately he had been going to Oakes more than LaMoure. Perhaps he was losing friends in LaMoure.

"This morning, I won the argument," she said, drawing my thoughts back into the room. With one arm, she embraced me; with the other, she smoothed her hair. "But he's bound to sell the grain soon. I wish I had followed Anton's advice, but how could I after Al read the letter from him?

"I want to wait to sell the grain. You know the big panic that started in August has affected prices. We might get more money for the crops if we wait to sell." She paused for a few moments.

"I just saw him head south," I volunteered.

"He'll no doubt be gone all day. Perhaps I had better sell the grain now, after all. Good prices or not, I'd have the money in hand."

I just stood patting her back, not knowing what to say or do. I thought about saddling up to go after George, who was boarding at a farm a few miles away.

Mother continued. "On the other hand, maybe Al is right. Maybe I am not thinking clearly. Maybe I need to trust him to be the head of our family."

"Huh!" I exclaimed. "Your thinker is working just fine when he isn't planting ideas in your head. I have come to believe he is a con artist. Don't let him take advantage of you."

Mother's resolve grew after she studied my eyes and saw that I meant what I said. She stood up heavily. "Go light a fire in the stove. I will wake your brothers up. We're going to have a busy day." She patted down her wild hairdo before going up the stairs.

I turned and went to the kitchen to put coal in the stove and light a fire. I was so thankful to be home that day. What if I had been staying at the Muirs? What would Mother have done?

We did the chores before we began loading both of our wagons with grain. Mother did not say a bad word about Al Roots to the boys, just that we needed to sell the grain immediately.

The boys rumbled out of the yard with the grain late in the morning. It was Saturday, and Carrie was home. The three of us began a nervous wait. The hours dragged on. None of us could keep our minds on our work, so we went to the parlor and tried to concentrate on our hand sewing.

It was four o'clock in the afternoon when the phone rang. Carrie dropped the rug she was working on and ran to answer it. Eddie was phoning to say they had sold the grain and he wanted permission to stay in town a while. Bill, now fourteen, was on his way home with the money.

Relieved, Mother began preparing sausage for supper as Carrie peeled potatoes. I put on my cloak and headed out the door. Bill would need help with the chores, so I might as well get started.

Just as I opened the door, Al Roots trotted past the house on his horse. I shrank back, closing the door. In the worst case of timing, Bill rattled into the driveway right behind him with the empty wagon. I opened the door and tried to flag him down, but he had seen Al and immediately headed to the barn. Al greeted my brother jovially as he took the horses' reigns and led them and the wagon into the barn.

I closed the door and turned to Mother.

"Mother, I think Al's been drinking," I said.

"Well, Bill will be starved. They'll be in soon enough to eat."

"But Bill's got the money from the sale," I reminded Mother.

"They should be coming to the house in a few minutes," Mother said, sounding less sure.

I looked at the clock in the dining room and began counting off minutes. "If they aren't in here in five minutes, no four minutes, I'm calling Gale." As I peered out the door again, a lantern light came on in the barn, and I could hear laughter. Then Bill pulled the door shut.

"I have a bad feeling about this. I'm going to call Gale and see if he'll pay a friendly visit," I said. Marching to the phone, I picked up the receiver and turned the crank.

"Please ring the Robert Muir residence," I said nervously to the operator.

When Mary Muir answered the phone, I asked for Gale. I had never called him before, so she must have known right away that something was not right.

"Of course, Bessie," she said, and I could hear her calling Gale. There were other voices in the background. My cheeks began to burn as I thought about the Muir family, probably with Janet and Albert, sitting around the table for a peaceful evening meal. I hated that my family seemed to leap from one shameful situation to the next. How would these kind people ever understand? Would Gale understand?

He came on the line moments later.

"Gale, I'm calling because you said if I ever needed your help…"

"Yes? What can I do?"

"Bill just came home. He and Eddie sold our grain today. He and Al Roots are out in the barn celebrating. I-I thought you might like to join the party." I tried to sound carefree, painfully aware that everyone in the neighborhood was probably rubbering on the party line.

"I'll be right over," Gale said, hanging up.

I turned and looked at Mother and nodded. She nodded back at me, relief in her eyes. For once, she would not have to fight her own battle.

"Will someone please tell me what's going on?" Carrie whined.

"Just another day in the Kloubec-Roots family," I answered dryly.

Gale arrived within minutes. I learned later he had just returned home and his horse was still saddled and ready to ride, which made for a quicker trip to our farm. I waited outside, wrapped against the early evening chill. Soon, he pulled up to the house, and I briefly told him what happened. He walked to the barn and opened the door.

"Say, what are you fellows up to?" he asked as he strolled purposefully in.

I could hear voices after that but could not make out what they were saying. I did not dare move any closer. Then the level of the voices went up a bit, and Bill hurried out of the barn. In the circle of light from the barn, I could see him carrying the bag with the grain money. Gale walked beside him, clapping him on the back, and talking low.

I smelled alcohol on Bill's breath as we went into the house together. Mother waited inside the door. "Bill, what was going on out there? Give me the grain money."

Bill turned over the bag, his head hanging a bit. "Aw, Al just offered me a toot. I didn't think you'd mind, since it was a big day and all."

Mother frowned at Bill and took the bag from his outstretched hands. "You're too young to drink, and you know it!" she said. Turning to Gale, she asked what he'd seen and heard.

"When I walked into the barn, Bill had the bottle. Al was saying, 'Now give me the bag in trade for my expensive elixir,'" Gale explained.

The door squeaked open, and the conversation stopped. Al Roots came in and bounded up the three steps into the kitchen. "Smells real good in here," he said. "Supper must be ready. Gale, you'll have to stay and eat with us." His words did not match the clench of his jaw. He hung his coat on a hook near the door and rubbed his hands together, giving Mother a scorching look.

The rest of us stood frozen like statues. He'd playacted with Mother before, making it look like she imagined things, but now all of us could clearly see the game he played. Gale stared at him, one eyebrow cocked, but Al met his gaze as though he had nothing to hide.

Mother responded first. "Get washed up. Dinner will be ready in five minutes," she said, disappearing with the bag of money. I was shocked that we were going to sit down for a meal together after Al Roots just tried to make off with a whole year's income. I could not believe it was happening any more than I could believe Father showed up that day long ago and acted as if he still lived at the farm.

Al chattered on as if nothing had happened, while the rest of us studied our plates. Perhaps we were searching for an explanation of Al Roots's bewildering actions. The queasy stomach I had had so often in Iowa came back, and I found myself unable to swallow much food.

Al Roots kept up a steady commentary. The food was good. Fresh garden carrots made the meal, yes sir! How were they cooked? Be sure to make them that way again. Boy, was it busy in Oakes today. That wind coming up from the east signaled a storm on the way. Mind you, the stronger the east wind, the bigger the storm. Batten down the hatches!

Mother remained calm, considering all that happened. I watched her across the table, my hand resting in Gale's beneath the table. By the set of her jaw, I figured Mother had her old starch back. She was weary but not defeated.

We all excused ourselves as soon as possible. Mother and Carrie cleaned up the supper dishes while I dallied outside with Gale. We walked around the farmyard whispering about the trials of the day. The sickening events seemed less important because my heart was thrilled by my gallant Gale. He had come to our rescue. Even if he had not given me the ring, my heart was settled. I knew he was the one for me.

Eddie came home about eight o'clock, and that was a good thing because no one had thought again to do the chores until he found the neglected animals. Gale and I hauled feed and water, while Eddie did the milking. By the time Gale left and I came back in the house, everyone had gone upstairs.

Carrie lay awake, waiting for me. She wanted to know when I first suspected Al Roots and how I knew there was a problem in the barn. We talked late into the night, and I finally told her all I knew.

Just as had happened many years ago, I heard noise in the yard toward morning. I slipped out of bed and looked out the window, shivering in my nightie. Al Roots was driving the team and wagon by the house.

I put on my robe and went downstairs in the dark. Mother stood silhouetted in the west window. I went to her and could see the strain on her face. I doubted she had slept much.

"Bessie," Mother whispered. "He's taking my team and leaving."

It seemed like a strange thing to say. They had been married for four years, and she still considered the property to be hers and not theirs. Was that part of the problem in their marriage?

Al Roots did not come home that day or night. The next day, I went to town with Gale, and we found the wagon and horses boarded at the livery stable. We asked at the train station, and yes, the station-master had sold a ticket to Mr. Roots. I took the team home, and the waiting game began.

We half-expected Al Roots to show up any day, pretending nothing was wrong. Mother would not say a word about him, but I noticed she sent someone to town almost every day to check around and get the mail.

Days stretched into weeks. Friends and neighbors asked about him, but what could we say? Well, I said he took a trip. Mother said he was away on business. Carrie said he left for good and was not welcome back. The boys seemed to avoid the topic as much as possible.

Meanwhile, the jeweler had sized my gold and pearl ring. How I wanted to wear it, but for now, it needed to stay safely hidden in my wicker basket, overshadowed by the latest family crisis.

35

If my desire to wear the engagement ring burned a hole in my heart, the question of whether to tell Gale about our other family secrets burned in my mind. For so many years, my family and I had managed to keep the door shut on our shameful past.

Starting fresh in Cottonwood Township gave all of us a second chance at life. Every day I rejoiced in the freedom brought by wiping the slate clean. Every week newcomers moved to the area. No one seemed to care about the past, except maybe Janet.

Although our neighbors accepted us, we knew that could change with one rumor about our parents' divorce or Joe living in an institution or our former ties to the Catholic church. But now we had another scandal. Al Roots! I thought hard about whether it was right to keep secrets from Gale or if I needed to confess our tangled past to him. What on earth would he think?

The whole Muir clan seemed as open as a Bible lying on a reading table. Upright. Normal. If Gale really knew me, would he accept me or would he break the engagement? I once again felt as though I were riding the seesaw at Grand Rapids Park. One moment I was up, feeling like the secrets did not matter, and the next minute I slammed to the ground, knowing I must tell Gale about everything before we married. While he had proven trustworthy in dealing with Al Roots, could he accept my painful past?

As it turned out, an opportunity to tell him everything opened up one nice fall day. With the harvest finished, Gale and I often went riding on the pretext of hunting prairie chickens or grouse. In truth, it was a way to be alone together.

One warm Indian summer day, we wandered north until we came to a place on the James River near Grand Rapids. I stopped Bump and slid off. "This is the most beautiful spot on earth," I declared. We sat down on a blanket I'd carried on the back of my saddle.

"Once you compared this valley to the Des Moines River Valley," Gale remembered. "That's about all I know about your life in Iowa. Why don't you talk more about the past?"

"There isn't much to tell. My mother's family, the Spireks, lived all over Webster County." I smiled remembering. "We had big family dinners, and we kids played baseball and had a lot of fun. At Christmas, we'd go to my uncle's place. They decorated the whole house, and we had music and food…" My thoughts trailed off, just thinking about those good days.

"Sounds like you have a lot to tell. Did your parents always farm?"

"They rented land until I was ten, and then they bought a farm."

"What was your father like?" Gale probed.

"He read the Bohemian newspaper to us after the evening meal. He did blacksmith work for the neighbors. He loved to tell jokes and could keep a crowd in stitches," I said, but in the back of my mind, I knew if I ever told Gale the truth, it had to be now.

"That is what 'twas like when I was young." I sighed. "But Father was hurt in an accident, and after that, he began drinking a lot. His temper got the best of him. And us.

"He left for a while and then came back. I thought things would be better when he moved back, but that didn't last long." I paused again, wondering if I dared go on.

"Do you want to know all of them? The family secrets?" I searched Gale's eyes. If I had seen the slightest flicker behind his pale eyelashes, I would have stopped right there. However, Gale held my gaze, urging me on without saying a word. I took a breath that sounded more ragged than I expected.

"The year 1899 was a very dark time for us. We were afraid of Father, with good reason. We could not predict his moods, and we all suffered from his meanness. My mother divorced him in 1900. The scandal shook up the whole Spirek family and was the talk of Webster

County. Mother's family was divided about whether the divorce was right, even though they had all seen her bruises. We were Catholic, and the church excommunicated her. It was an awful time."

"I had no idea."

"Then we've whitewashed the past pretty well."

"What happened to your father?" Gale asked. "Wait, are you saying he's still alive? I always thought he died."

I gave Gale a rueful smile. "We skirt the truth by saying he's gone. Sometimes I almost believe it. But my aunt, Annie Spirek, wrote that he still lives in the area and works for a farmer there. He pretty much lost everything in the divorce. Aunt Annie has heard…things. She said he may end up in a mental institution." Speaking those words hurt as much as if someone had sliced out part of my heart.

Gale remained silent. I literally held my breath, listening to the breeze rustle the tall dried grass. Then finally, I took a deep breath. "There is more. Our family has many secrets. I have a brother named Joe."

Gale twirled his watch chain and looked out at the river. My heart sank. No doubt this information would ruin any possibility of a future together. Yet telling the truth felt right.

"Joe lives at a state-run home, the Iowa Institution for Feeble-Minded Children. He is two years older than I am. He lived with us until I was twelve. They sent him away before the divorce."

Gale looked at me now and tried to cover my hand with his, but I shook it off as my words rushed out. "Mother couldn't handle the farm, so she sold it and managed a boarding house. We lived there in Moreland for four years. We worked night and day at that boarding house. Then Mother met Al Roots, and they got married. We left our old life behind when we moved here, but as you know, the family misery continues. I couldn't let you marry me without knowing the truth about Iowa."

I looked off over the valley before us and pushed my glasses further up my nose. "I blamed myself for a long time. If I'd been a better daughter, a better sister." My voice wavered, and I stopped talking for a minute and tried to breathe deep. Finally I continued. "Now I know that it was not my fault, but my family is tainted by the past. I wouldn't blame you a bit if you returned to that scandal-free fiancée in Minnesota!"

There, I had confessed the truths that plagued me night and day. They would break us apart or bind us together. Either way, I knew telling Gale was the right thing to do.

He remained silent for a long time while I tore out the grass next to me by the roots. I could feel my heart thumping in my chest, and I vaguely tried to imagine life without this gentle, gallant man.

"Well, I guess we better be going," he finally said as he stood up, dusted off his pants, and plopped his hat on his head. I looked up at him. The sun was behind him, and I could only see his silhouette.

"I wouldn't blame you—" I began, but Gale cut me off.

"Bessie, I'm grateful you've told me your secrets. I knew there was something wrong, and I wondered how we could be man and wife if you were not honest with me. But you know I have been crazy about you ever since the first day I saw you. Let's let the past stay in the past, together."

"Oh, Gale," I peered up at him. "Do you mean it?"

"I sure do. You do not need to keep any secrets from me. We're in this together."

He pulled me up and put his arms around me. I swallowed back a lump in my throat and blinked away tears that had suddenly sprung up. We stood looking out over the stunning view of the James River winding through the valley thick with bare-branched trees and dotted with little farms.

The view seemed a good sign for the future, as good as having this gallant man for a husband.

36

November 1907

The topic of Al Roots was a closed subject. Another month went by before Carrie and I dared quiz Mother about him. She finally admitted he had packed her good valise with his clothes the morning he left. She did not expect him back. We should, she said with determination, carry on as though he had never existed. If someone asked, he had extended business in Missouri.

I missed Al Roots like I would miss a rock in my shoe, so I took Mother at her word, prepared to move on with my life. The symbol of a happy future lay tucked in my bureau drawer.

The Sunday before Thanksgiving, I took my engagement ring to church. After the service as we sat outside in the schoolyard, Gale slipped it on my finger again. "Bessie Emma Kloubec, will you please marry me soon?" he asked.

"Yes, Gale Andrew Muir, I will!" I said, stroking the smooth tiny pearls and looking into his eyes, which seemed to be the same vivid blue as the November sky.

"I don't want to wait anymore," he said. "But I'd like the reverend to marry us and not a justice of the peace."

"Me too," I said. Mother had twice been married by a justice of the peace, and I was not about to begin my new life following her way. "Let's go back in and ask him if he'll do it. Maybe we can set a date."

A hush had settled over the inside of the school as buggies and automobiles wheeled out of the driveway. We walked inside and saw

Reverend Nordewier sitting quietly in the front row, seemingly lost in thought or prayer. Gale coughed, and the genial man with the shiny pate turned and waved at us. We walked toward the front.

"Reverend Nordewier, we want you to be the first to know. I've asked this young lady to be my bride, and she said yes!"

"Well, this is a surprise! And a nice one," he said.

"We're wondering if you would do the honor of marrying us?" Gale asked anxiously, cutting through the small talk.

"Of course I'll marry you. Are you thinking of a large wedding?"

A shadow crossed Gale's face, and he turned to me with a questioning look. I had not thought much about the ceremony. My thoughts were of waking up with Gale each morning and spending every day for the rest of our lives together.

I pulled my thoughts back to the present moment as I heard the good reverend saying, "—seats forty people. Of course, if you want a larger wedding, we can hold it in LaMoure at the town church. The reception and dinner could be at the Windsor Hotel. With the new expansion this year, it certainly is a grand place to celebrate a wedding. Imagine, gas lights and a dining room that seats over ninety people."

I looked at Gale and thought of the big wedding his first fiancée wanted. He preferred something simple. With family scandals hanging over the Kloubec household, so did I. If we did have a big wedding, the invitation list would include hundreds of friends, neighbors, and relatives. And the food! I knew Mother could not afford a meal at the Windsor. Her pocketbook had been dented by Al Roots's dealings, not to mention how nervous everyone was about banks closing around the country. People were already calling it the Panic of 1907.

If we did all the work for the wedding ourselves and held it, say, at the school, it would take a whole beef or a flock of chickens to feed the crowd, not to mention weeks of preparation. Furthermore, our parents did not even know we were getting married yet! Gale turned his hat around, pinching the brim between his thumbs and forefingers as he watched me.

"Sir, we want a simple wedding," I said. Beside me, Gale let out a sigh of relief.

I brainstormed as I talked. "Is there any reason we couldn't be married on Christmas Day? We would like a simple service at my home, with just family present. We could make it part of the Christmas celebration." I could see in Gale's eyes that he liked the idea.

Reverend Nordewier spoke first. "Why, Bessie, I think that's a fine idea. I'd be happy to perform the ceremony at your home."

"Then it's settled," said Gale. "We can work out the details in the coming weeks."

We stopped at the Muir farm next and told Gale's family the news. There were hugs and congratulations all around. Janet even volunteered to make the wedding cake. I was going to love being part of the Muir family.

We arrived at our farm just as Mother took a pan of scalloped potatoes out of the oven. She frowned at me because I had not come home right after church to help with dinner preparations. For once I did not care; I just gave her a big silly smile as she quickly ushered us to the dining room table. After we were seated, I lifted my water glass with my left hand, flashing my ring.

Within moments, Carrie saw it and gasped. "Bessie, where did you get that ring?" All eyes turned to me. I held my hand higher.

"Gale asked me to marry him. I said yes!"

My brothers began banging on the table and shouting. Carrie's mouth worked, but no sound came out. Mother seemed stunned for a moment, but she soon recovered. She shushed the boys, and the room fell silent. "I guess I should have expected this," she said calmly. "Congratulations. When do you plan to get married?"

37

December 1907

I stepped into a storybook world that December.

Mother, Carrie, and I worked together to make my wedding dress, enjoying each other's company as we discussed plans for the big day. I no longer felt the antagonism toward my mother that I had wrestled with back when I was eleven and thought I was so grown up. Mother was not an easy person, but she had overcome many painful difficulties and she now had my respect.

Still, we all sensed the bittersweet reality that our times together like this were ending. I planned to move in with the Muirs after the wedding. In the spring, Robert and Mary Muir would move into town, and the farm would be ours.

"Something old, something new, something borrowed, something blue," Carrie chirped. "That's what they now say every bride should have."

I had lots of "something new." For my wedding dress, we ordered lovely crepe fabric in a soft cream color. Working together, we laid out the material on the dining room table and cut around the pattern. I sewed much of it on the sewing machine, while Mother and Carrie did the handwork.

The dress fit me perfectly and showed off all our fancy sewing skills. It had a high neck and bloused bodice. The bishop sleeves narrowed at the elbow and ended in wide cuffs. The skirt fell from the wide shirred belt into a five-gore skirt with graceful folds from the knee.

Along with the dress, Mother insisted that I order a new corset, bustle, hose, and shoes. Selecting shoes became my hardest decision. Kid, felt, or patent leather? I threw practicality out the window and ordered patent-leather sandals. Later I regretted not getting a pair of felt high-tops that would have kept my feet warmer.

For "something borrowed," I carried a lace handkerchief that Aunt Annie sent in the mail just for the occasion. She had carried it at her own wedding. Later I sent it back to her so her daughters could use it when they walked down the aisle someday. To my embarrassment, Carrie gave me "something blue." It made me turn red to think of wearing lacey blue garters, but I wore them anyway.

I decided right away to carry the triangular veil from Father as "something old," but I was not sure how to explain it to Mother. As it turned out, I did not need to. I wrapped it around the silk bride roses that I held during the ceremony. No one even noticed it.

I felt Father's presence in the little veil and, just for a moment, longed for what could not be. On Christmas Eve, I wrapped the roses in the veil and shed a few tears, wishing Father could give me away on my wedding day. I imagined him driving up just before the wedding wearing a top hat and a big smile. He would wink at me, take my arm, and stand with me before the preacher, then he would place my hand in Gale's as he took his place at my side.

A sigh escaped me as I let go of the wistful vision and returned to reality. I needed to be grateful for the best big brother in the world. George would do the honors at the wedding.

That night, Carrie and I whispered under the covers for the last time. After she drifted off to sleep, her breathing slow and steady like a softly played violin, I lay awake thinking about the big day ahead. It occurred to me that I was getting married on the Lord's birthday.

The thought took me back seven years to my eleventh birthday, the day our family started falling apart. Since then, every choice had seemed risky. Now I was making a choice meant to last all my life, the choice that had failed my mother twice. Yet I could not imagine not marrying Gale. I had to take the risk. I had to take the risk and trust God on this one. Just as surely as if I put a present at His feet, I handed my future to God, faith wrapped in hope.

38

When I awoke on Christmas morning, the dawn of a bright, clear day shone through the dormer window. Rather than bounding out of bed as I usually did, I lingered, savoring the wonder of the moment. My wedding day had finally arrived! I was nineteen years old, Gale was twenty-three, and every uncertainty about this decision had been erased.

When I went downstairs, the aroma of roasting meats greeted me, although the morning was still young. Mother was setting the dining room table with the good china. We had decked the long living and dining room with fragrant spruce boughs entwined with red ribbons and pinecones from the north shelterbelt.

I chose the southeast corner of the living room to stand with Gale before God and man. Reverend Nordewier arrived right after the Christmas morning service at Cottonwood Church. Mr. and Mrs. Muir and Janet and Albert Hunt were right behind him. They, along with my family, made the wedding party complete.

As the company entered the house, we called out the Bohemian Christmas greeting of "Vesele Vanoce!" They responded with the Scottish greeting of "Blithe Yule!" Everyone laughed and talked, enjoying the sweet traditions on this most holy day. Speaking the happy greeting in my native tongue brought back the joyful feelings I had as a child greeting my Spirek family so long ago in Iowa.

Gale looked as nervous as I felt. I could not decide if he looked cute or handsome with his coppery red hair slicked back and sporting a white bow tie. I took his hand and squeezed it. Mother played Bach before the simple ceremony began.

We took our places beneath an archway of greenery. Through the east window, the serene white snowscape offered itself as a gift on this special day. To Gale's joy, a flock of pheasants dallied there, picking at corn strewn from the corncrib.

I could hardly breathe, but for once, it was because I was happy rather than fearful or anxious. My oldest brother, George, gave me away. Carrie was my bridesmaid. After we said our "I do's" Mother struck the first bright note of Mendelssohn's "Wedding March," and everyone clapped. Gale kissed me, and we both blushed.

Then we sat down to a feast of blended traditions—oyster stew, roasted goose, turkey, potatoes, gravy, pickled beets, Scottish shortbread, mincemeat pie, and kolaches.

During the meal, Gale stood to his feet and raised his glass to me. "To my Bessie, brave and beautiful, who is really mine today." Everyone raised their glasses with him as I sat awash in the pleasure of the moment. George stood and welcomed Gale to the family with great seriousness rather than his usual comic comments. And for once, Carrie's tongue was tied.

Janet had baked a three-layer wedding cake, frosted white with loops and flowers and topped with red frosting roses. It was so pretty I hated to cut it, but it tasted even better than it looked. After the meal, we opened wedding gifts from our families. I especially remember the pretty things, including a china plate and a cut-glass water pitcher.

Then suddenly, it was time for George to hitch up the cutter. He and Carrie planned to drive us to the train station. I rushed upstairs and put on my blue traveling suit.

Mother stayed at the farm to see the guests off and begin cleaning up. She offered me a reserved good-bye hug, and she shook Gale's hand real hard. How I wished for a big hug from her, but it would never be. As a girl, I thought her actions cold, but now the woman in me could see her struggling to maintain her emotions. I was the first of her brood to marry.

We arrived in LaMoure as the Northern Pacific rumbled to the train station. Steam billowed so thick it was hard to see. We did not have much time for farewells. Gale ran into the station to purchase the tickets, and George hoisted the bags down from the wagon. I looked at my valise, hoping I remembered to pack everything. I was taking my wedding dress, in addition to a couple of shirtwaists and a black skirt. My new white nightie lay hidden in the bottom of the bag.

"Bessie," Carrie said close to my ear. The noise from the train made it hard to hear. "Last time we were at the train station together, we had just arrived here, ready to make a new life. And here you are making another new start." I just nodded, unable to speak lest I begin to cry.

Her own eyes momentarily filled with tears, and then her expression changed. She grabbed me away from the others and whispered in all seriousness, "Do you know what to do on your wedding night?"

I just stared at her for a moment. *Oh, leave it to Carrie*, I thought!

"Don't worry, we'll figure it out," I whispered back. She squeezed my hand, pressing in a small bottle of perfume.

"For your wedding night!" she whispered. "You can tell me all about it."

"Thank you for the perfume," I murmured. "But don't expect any particulars about our honeymoon."

Turning away, I found George approaching, looking into my eyes. I could see his heart was as full as mine. He gave me a big bear hug.

"George, you're the best big brother ever. Thanks for all the advice through the years and for always being there for me." I smiled, even though I could feel tears well up in my eyes.

"God be with you, Bessie."

"And with you, George. Always with you," I said.

Gale came out of the station with the tickets in his hand. He shook George's hand and took my elbow. Carrie patted my arm one last time.

Then we climbed the train steps and sat on the green velvet seats looking out at the station. Spying George and Carrie, we smiled and waved. The rumble of the train engine increased, and we lurched forward. The few buildings east of the station began to drift by.

We sank back in our seats, hand in hand. After the busyness of the day, I could feel the starch go out of Gale. He relaxed and put his arm around me as we whispered together, awed that we were now husband and wife. Finally, he lay his head on my shoulder and dozed off.

The quiet moments that followed gave me a little time to reflect on the idea of being married. I could hardly believe we'd taken this big step. I gratefully remembered how far I had come. Not so long ago, my fears and unforgiveness had bound me to the past, and I tried to avoid any chance of being hurt again. Only when I grew desperate with the dismal state of my heart did I seek advice from Aunt Annie.

I would always remember her words: *I pray you will always have the peace of God in your heart. In my own life, I find the key to peace is forgiving others and forgiving myself.*

The anger in my heart was swept away that day, making room for the future. Not only had I been set free from fear and anger, now Gale and I would face the future together.

As we rolled through the countryside, joy engulfed me, and the sun shone prettily on the bare trees silhouetted against the snow. Little farms and villages and frozen rivers and lakes along the track looked like an artist's idea of perfection. Even the rolling hills, which later flattened as we entered the Red River Valley, looked more beautiful than I'd ever seen before.

The vibrant scene was a gift from God that I will never forget, and it caused a tune to begin roaming through my head, one we often sang in church. I hummed through the first verse:

> *This is my Father's world,*
> *And to my listening ears*
> *All nature sings, and round me rings*
> *The music of the spheres.*
> *This is my Father's world:*
> *I rest me in the thought*
> *Of rocks and trees, of skies and seas;*
> *His hand the wonders wrought.*

My heart rang with joy at the words, but when I came to the third verse, it felt like God himself was speaking to me:

This is my Father's world.
O let me ne'er forget
That though the wrong seems oft so strong,
God is the ruler yet.
This is my Father's world:
why should my heart be sad?
The Lord is King; let the heavens ring!
God reigns; let the earth be glad.

All my growing-up years, I had wondered how to make good choices. I still didn't have a pat answer to my big question, but a peace settled over me. My heavenly Father would see me through. Though the wrong often seemed strong, He still reigned, and knowing that filled the longing I had for a father on whom I could rely.

In addition, I was traveling toward a new life with a man whom I trusted and loved, a man who shared the secrets locked away in the dark closet of my heart.

Outside the window, the earth did seem glad. And, tucked in next to my beloved, so was I.

Postscript

Hardy folks that we were, Gale and I went to Minnesota for a two-week winter honeymoon. In the Twin Cities, we had wedding photos taken. Gale wore his dark suit and white bow tie, and I had on my ivory wedding dress. We were supposed to look stern, but I was giddy with happiness and could not help smiling into the camera.

We visited family and went sightseeing in Minneapolis before taking the train to Jackson, Minnesota. There I met the rest of Gale's family. By then, winter had set in for good. Each day, we visited different relatives. His brothers, sisters, and their families clearly adored Gale, and they warmly welcomed me as we talked, ate, and played games. When we left Jackson, I felt very much a part of the Muir family.

Bessie and Gale Muir Wedding photo, 1907

Chapter Notes

Chapter 1: Documents found a century later included a doctor's report stating that Vincent Kloubec said he'd been kicked in the head and back by a horse. There was no indication of when this happened. The document is in the Muir-Kloubec records stored at the North Dakota Heritage Center in Bismarck.

Chapter 3: Bessie told the author she had less than an eighth grade education. In her oral history, Carrie Kloubec Brandes said Bessie had completed sixth grade.

A photo album was discovered in 2013 by Bessie Kloubec Muir's great-granddaughter. Bessie had written her name and the date in it.

Chapter 4: Most of Mary Spirek Kloubec Roots's siblings were buried at Graceland Cemetery, Webster County, Iowa, but others were buried at the Catholic cemetery in Fort Dodge, indicating some stayed in the Catholic Church when they moved to America, but others left.

Chapter 7: Bessie gave the author an aged triangle of lace in the 1960s. Where she obtained it and whether she used it when attending mass as a girl are matters of speculation.

Chapter 8: The Fort Museum in Fort Dodge has a frontier village set in the era in which Bessie lived, prompting ideas for the family's furnishings. The general store has a scale like the one described here.

Chapter 9: In 1899, Bessie's brother Joseph Kloubec was sent to the Iowa Institute for the Feebleminded at Glenwood.

Chapter 11: Carrie Kloubec Brandes recorded her oral history in about 1980. The story about the hair and the curling iron were in it.

Chapter 12: Vincent and Mary Kloubec's divorce hearing took place on January 19, 1900, at the Webster County Courthouse. Mary was awarded the farm, plus most of the equipment. Vincent received a cash settlement of $900, plus $400 worth of livestock and equipment.

An old handgun was found in Bessie's dark closet when she died in August 1966. The origin of the gun as well its make and model are unknown.

Chapter 13: Wallace Muir said relatives in Iowa recalled that Vincent went to the farm after the divorce and Mary was frightened enough to walk to the neighbors in winter and stay overnight. Vincent stayed at the farm overnight, and Bessie fed him break-fast before he left. He took Mary's horse and buggy. Mary then had a restraining order issued against him.

Chapter 15: That Mary was excommunicated by the Catholic Church is speculative.

Mary managed a boarding house for railroad officials in Moorland for four years during a railroad boom. In 2010, the author found a large two-story house for sale in Moorland. When contacted, the owner stated that it was thought to have been a boarding house at one time.

Carrie's son, Warren Brandes, recalled that his mother told her children that she almost died when she was ten of either scarlet fever or diphtheria. The doctor treated her for the wrong disease, but she survived. Apparently she stayed with relatives during her recovery.

Chapter 16: Mary married W. A. Roots on October 13, 1903, in Rockwell City, Iowa.

Chapter 17: Mary purchased a 320-acre farm in Cottonwood Township (now Dean Township) near LaMoure, North Dakota on December 22, 1903. The family moved from Iowa to North Dakota in March of 1904.

Chapter 18: In her oral history, Carrie Kloubec Brandes said that word of a new family in the neighborhood spread by party line: "The newcomers are here, and they have five kids!"

Chapter 19: Carrie's oral history recalled how the neighbors surprised Bessie with a sixteenth birthday party.

Chapter 21: In the oral history, Carrie said the family didn't plant a crop in 1904, but Mary did plant peanuts, along with other garden plants, and that there was a hard freeze on August 16.

Decades later, Carrie and the author's mother posed for a photo by a spirea in full bloom next to a stucco house. Whether it was the farmhouse is conjecture.

For many years after the property was sold, Mary's descendants were invited to harvest the chokecherry and apricot trees from the shelterbelt north of the farmstead.

Chapter 22: Cottonwood Presbyterian Church was organized on March 26, 1905, with twenty-seven charter members. They met at the school until 1917, when a church was built a few miles southwest of the school. Information obtained from *A History of LaMoure, 1882–1982.*

Chapter 23: Her mother gave Bessie a Morgan horse and a buggy for her eighteenth birthday, the equivalent of receiving a new car. The horse's name was Bump.

At age sixteen, Carrie attended college in Valley City for six weeks, received her teacher's certificate, and began teaching at one of the Dean Township schools.

Chapter 24: Gale Muir's brother, John, moved to LaMoure in 1906 and enticed many of his family members to buy land in the area.

Chapter 25: Bessie worked for Robert and Mary Muir when they moved to Cottonwood Township in 1906. Carrie told the story about the ice cream episode in Grand Rapids in her oral history. The Muirs's daughter, Janet, lived nearby with her husband, Albert Hunt. She had a reputation in the family of being kind but rather straitlaced.

Chapter 26: Gale enjoyed hunting all his life. Robert Crawford Muir wrote this original story called "A Night in a Snowbank" which is recorded in the Muir-Kloubec history.

In her oral history, Carrie told of getting lost in a snowstorm and how her horse found the way home.

Chapter 27: All her life, Bessie gave food to drifters who knocked on the door looking for a meal; whether they reminded her of her father is speculation.

Carrie made braided rugs all her life. The tradition of rug-making was passed down to other women in the family.

Chapter 28: As reported in the *Muir-Kloubec History*, Gale was engaged to a pastor's daughter from Jackson when he moved to LaMoure, but broke it off after meeting Bessie. The fiancée apparently returned the ring, which was given to Aileen Muir Simpson when she graduated from high school.

Chapter 32: The words to the song "Paper of Pins" were around at least as far back as the nineteenth century, and it was familiar in the British Islands and Canada. The Four Lads recorded it in the 1950s. That Gale sang it is conjecture.

Chapter 33: The gold and pearl ring is still in the family.

Chapter 34: Mary's marriage to Al Roots had disintegrated by 1907. The *Muir-Kloubec History* reported that he did try to take the crop money and that Bessie did phone Gale asking for help.

Chapter 35: Gale apparently kept Bessie's secrets. His son, Wallace Muir, may have been the only person with whom he discussed the Kloubec secrets. Their conversation took place after Wallace returned from World War II. Wallace didn't expose them for over fifty years, until he had documented the events of 1899 through 1907.

Chapter 36: Al Roots did take the team into LaMoure, left them at the livery stable, and boarded the train never to return. This became another family secret. When the 1920 census records were opened seventy two years later, Wallace Muir found a record of Roots living with a wife and a stepson in Missouri.

Chapter 37: Bessie's wedding dress may be seen in her wedding photo.

Chapter 38: Bessie and Gale married in the southeast corner of the farmhouse. Walter and Amanda Ubben purchased the farm; Amanda once showed the author the spot where the marriage took place. They took the train to Minnesota for their honeymoon. *This is My Father's World, Maltbie Davenport Babcock, 1901*

Addendum

Although *Secrets of the Dark Closet* closes in 1907 with the marriage of Bessie Kloubec and Gale Muir, the story really didn't end there. This addendum gives a brief summary of the lives of the Kloubec family. Admittedly, the information is cherry-picked to give an overview. Several of Bessie's siblings had stories engaging enough to merit their own stories. I hope they are told someday.

All the following information was taken from the *Muir-Kloubec Genealogy & History*. The direct quotes by author Wallace G. Muir appear in italics.

Vincent Kloubec by Wallace Muir: *"I am not sure that Bessie was fully aware of her father's fate. In 1908, he was committed to the Cherokee State Mental Hospital in Cherokee, Iowa. His examination prior to his commitment revealed that he was moody and would not respond to questions and was mourning the loss of his farm. Nowadays he would have been medicated for depression before commitment to an institution. He remained confined to the mental institution until 1916, at which time he was transferred to the Webster County Poor Farm. Vincent died at the Poor Farm on April 22, 1933. His body was transferred to the University of Iowa School of Medicine for use as a cadaver by the students in training. After his body served its useful purpose in the medical school, it was cremated and place with other 'cremains' in a common grave. His death certificate was hard to find, since his last name had been misspelled on the document. My hired researcher accidentally discovered his death certificate during a search for other information in the Webster County Courthouse. His name was spelled "Kolbeck" rather than Kloubec, but I was able to ascertain that it was his certificate from other information and a letter I had received from Iowa University.*

This is Gayle again. In 2010, my husband and I spent some time in Iowa doing research. One day as we drove west on Highway 20, we happened past a red-brick institution near Fort Dodge. It was now a Baptist seminary, but a sign explained that one tall brick building was the original Webster County Poor Farm. We'd accidentally found the place where Vincent Kloubec spent his final days. Ironically, his in-laws lived on the property adjacent to the Poor Farm, meaning Vincent would have been reminded daily of the loss of his family and farm, two things most precious to him. The humiliating descent of Vincent's life began with an apparent addiction to alcohol at a time when it was seen as a weakness rather than a disease.

Mary Kloubec Roots: Eventually Mary bought a house in LaMoure, North Dakota, and moved to town, where she lived with her daughter Carrie and her husband, Carl Brandes. Mary had a good head for business, was a finely skilled seamstress, and had a talent for growing things, attributes she passed on to her descendants. In 1919, Mary had a stroke and became bedridden. She died December 5, 1923, at the age of fifty-eight and is buried in Rosehill Cemetery at LaMoure.

George Kloubec: Bessie remained close to her oldest brother all his life. He married Maud Montgomery in 1912, and they farmed along the LaMoure and Dickey County line, south of Mary Roots's farm. According to a granddaughter, they were an active part of the young rural community and took pride in their farm. They purchased a kit house and assembled it on site. Sadly, Maud was a victim of the influenza epidemic of 1918, although she lived until 1930. George juggled farming and caring for her and their three children. George died on August 12, 1954. The farm was still in the family in 2016.

Joseph Kloubec by Wallace Muir: *In 1899, Mary and Vincent committed their son Joseph to the Home for Feeble-Minded Children in Glenwood, Iowa. None of the available records indicate the exact nature of his disability, but later information suggests that it may have been epilepsy. In 1900, epilepsy had little or no treatment available to ease a sufferer's convulsions. This strongly affected the other children, and it became a deep, dark secret they withheld even from their own families. That was not the age of enlightenment.*

Joseph Kloubec lived at Glenwood for twenty-five years. Records show he only had two visitors in that time; his mother and his sister Carrie each visited once. Later he was transferred to the Woodward State School for epileptics, where he lived another twenty-six years. Bessie and Carrie secretly sent packages to him until his death on November 26, 1951. To avoid questions from their children, they probably conferred with each other in Bohemian.

Bessie Kloubec Muir: After marrying on Christmas Day 1907, Bessie and Gale Muir farmed for a few years then moved into LaMoure, where Gale worked mostly as a carpenter. They had nine children and raised eight to adulthood. They lived through the death of their daughter June at age two, World War I, the Dust Bowl, Depression, and World War II, in which all four of their sons served. Their other children were Neva, Margaret, Donald, Aileen, Wallace, Willis, Robert and Betty. After Gale died in 1957, Bessie continued to live in the small house they bought in 1922. Until her death on August 31, 1966, she maintained five gardens each summer and spent winters at the treadle sewing machine given to her by Gale's brother Bob as a wedding gift. There indeed was a closet off the kitchen called the "dark closet." A granddaughter purchased that house, and has opened the Muir Guest House in another home they owned.

Carrie Kloubec Brandes: Carrie married a LaMoure business-man, Carl Brandes, in 1913. She was a career woman in an era when most women were housewives. She taught school and worked along-side Carl at the Brandes and Foran general store. The couple had four children and cared for Mary Roots in her declining years. Carl died while out hunting in 1944. Carrie took over his job as postmaster at LaMoure. During this time, all her children received college edu-cations. Later, she was appointed director of the LaMoure County Selective Service, an office she held for the next twenty-five years, retiring at age seventy-five. She had an avid interest in professional baseball, politics, and world affairs all her life. Carrie died on April 13, 1981, at the age of ninety-two.

Edwin Kloubec: Edwin was a musician in the Navy during World War I. He lived most of his adult life in California where, among other things, he was a musician in the U.S. Army Cavalry.

Edwin never married, and little is known about him. He died on October 10, 1949. After a Christian Science memorial service at LaMoure, his ashes were buried at Rosehill Cemetery.

William (Bill) Kloubec: Bill also served in World War I. He was wounded in France and received the Purple Heart and Silver Star. He graduated from the University of North Dakota in 1925 and was part owner of the Gambles Store and had rental properties in Fargo, North Dakota and a farm in Minnesota. He and his wife, Vera Pomeroy, had two children. He died in Fargo on April 15, 1959.

—Gayle Larson Schuck

About the Author

Gayle Larson Schuck grew up at LaMoure and now lives at Bismarck, North Dakota. She worked in public relations and development as a prelude to becoming an author. Gayle has taught Bible classes for over 30 years, and can often be found in the public library looking for books, or attending her writers' group and book club. Times spent with her family along the Missouri River are among her treasured moments.

Read more about the author on her website and blog: www.gaylelarsonschuck.com.

www.ingramcontent.com/pod-product-compliance
Lightning Source LLC
Chambersburg PA
CBHW021152110726
47900CB00002B/530